HelenKay Dimon
VICTORIA'S GOT A SECRET

LIFE . . . ROMANTICIZED

HelenKay Dimon
VICTORIA'S GOT A SECRET

Health Communications, Inc.
Deerfield Beach, Florida

www.hcibooks.com

Library of Congress Cataloging-in-Publication Data

HelenKay Dimon.
   Victoria's got a secret / HelenKay Dimon.
      p. cm.
   ISBN-13: 978-0-7573-1557-2
   ISBN-10: 0-7573-1557-7
   ISBN-13: 978-0-7573-9182-8
   ISBN-10: 0-7573-9182-6
I. Women television journalists—Fiction.   I. Title.
   PS3604.I467V53 2011
   813'.6—dc22

                                                 2011002606

Publisher: Health Communications, Inc.
3201 S.W. 15th Street
Deerfield Beach, FL 33442–8190

TRUE VOWS Series Developer: Olivia Rupprecht
Cover photo ©iStockphoto
Cover design by Larissa Hise Henoch
Interior design and formatting by Lawna Patterson Oldfield

Prologue

THIS TIME WAS DIFFERENT. She made the decisions and set the boundaries. The days of acting out someone else's fantasy faded into the shadowed past. Her new life focused on *taking* control.

Her body. Her mind. Her choices.

She could stay or leave, and she chose to stay. The new office, complete with the impressive title and growing responsibilities, proved that. So did the thick stack of papers sitting on the edge of her desk.

Without thinking, she traced her fingertip over the signature line of the employment contract and didn't fight the smile. The blue ink had dried days ago but the unspoken statement she'd made still pounded in her brain.

She'd spent the first part of her career with Naked News building an image and creating a persona. Becoming *the* Victoria Sinclair. In interviews back then, she spoke about how women taking off their clothes as they delivered the news was the perfect mix of pretty women and information.

She had believed the words, the concept, and most certainly in the people who ran Naked News. She had used her numerous talk show appearances and private dinners to plead her case to those she knew and those she didn't. But in some ways she'd only said the words. Now she lived them.

Victoria Sinclair went from a role she played to something more. A piece of the whole. The part that found strength from within and knowledge from life as well as the pages of books. She'd once hidden behind the persona, then she repressed it. Now she would nurture it, understanding the power and the need to harness it.

Her grandmother, known to the family as The Duchess, taught her to respect her body and use her mind. The Duchess insisted a woman could be anything and didn't have to give up part of her soul to accomplish her goals.

The Duchess was right.

One

You don't choose love. Love chooses you.

—Grandma Gladys, The Duchess

SHE'D SEEN HIM AROUND ST. CLAIR'S SECONDARY school. Blondish-brown hair swept long over his ears, giving him the look of a sexy brooding musician despite his wide smile. He was the guy who got along with everyone, moving from the jock crowd to the popular crowd to the artsy crowd with ease.

His name was Paul, and he was a year older. A touch of mystery surrounded him, which made him all the more attractive. Nothing like a guy with a bit of experience and access to a car to make him interesting. Being cute didn't hurt either.

Jennifer pegged him as charming with a bit of the devil in his sparkling green eyes. But touching him was the memory that stuck with her. Lean fingers and a firm hold. The moment came from ninth grade when the gym teacher paired them up in square dancing.

Jogging over to her, he wore a leather vest and faded blue jeans that hugged his thighs and showed off his love of sports and physical activity. His arm slipped through hers and her stomach bounced. She'd kissed a boy at camp once, but this, the skin against skin contact, sucked the air right out of her.

1

With Paul, swinging around in a circle didn't seem silly or embarrassing. The world whirled around her as they clapped and stepped. She wanted the dance to last forever.

But this meeting months later was different. No laughing students or dumb music. They were alone in his room.

Her big sister Heather usually agreed to have her tag along on social stuff, but this time Heather had wanted to be with her boyfriend. It was New Year's Eve, after all. Being dumped would have sucked for Jennifer if Heather hadn't done a little matchmaking and arranged for the dumping to happen at Paul's house.

Snow fell outside as cold air blew off Lake Huron and wrapped around Sarnia, the harbor city in southern Ontario where they lived. Pink Floyd echoed off the walls of the dark basement.

After hours of talking about his most recent hike and the bands he liked best, of her talking about her offbeat family and its focus on learning and reading, they took a long breath and looked up. Hours had passed as they sat locked together, hands touching and heads bent in conversation.

She knew he was different from the boys at school. He listened, looked at her like her words mattered, and seemed to understand her better than any boy she'd ever met.

To break the spell she felt weaving around her, she glanced around the sparse underground space. No one had bothered them. No parents to separate them or demand she head home. If this were her house, her dad would have checked in more than once by now. Probably would have lingered around until he scared Paul off.

But nothing about the room or the moment reminded of her of her usual life. She lived in a house with books stacked in every corner and on every shelf and a piano at its center. Her days were filled with music and heated discussions where she took one side and her mom took another.

Paul's surroundings carried a note of loneliness. Quiet and dark. Stuffing peeked out of the frayed edges of the pillows. The rug was worn through to the cement below in a several places. The stacked stereo looked like it cost more than everything else in the room combined.

"Where is everybody?" she asked.

"Out."

A typical Paul response, short and a bit cryptic but spoken with laughter in his voice. "That's specific."

"Meaning?"

"You're here by yourself?"

"No."

"Really?"

He gave her a you're-losing-it look. "You're here."

"Oh, right." Her gaze lingered on the bed before returning to his face. "Your parents let you sleep down here?"

"Yeah."

"Alone?"

"I like privacy," he said, not really answering the question.

"What's this?" She stood up and went to the odd assortment of treasures lined up on top of his dresser. Her fingers brushed over each item.

"Nothing."

She grabbed his sleeve when he started to turn away. "No, really. Tell me."

He shrugged. "Do you really care?"

As if there was anything about him that didn't matter to her. She doodled his name in her notebook, and just seeing his face in the halls at school made her stomach bounce around with excitement.

Yeah, she cared. Like, couldn't stop thinking about him cared. "Just tell me."

Still he stayed quiet. He bit his lip. Even frowned at her. Finally, he cleared his throat and started talking. "It's all the stuff that matters."

"Oh." She hesitated, then shook her head. "Yeah, I don't get it."

He picked up the stone chips and fingered the dried rose with a reverence that made him seem years older than sixteen. "From Marie's grave."

Pain washed through his voice as he talked. His usually sunny face pulled tight with a grim line across his lips.

Jennifer knew the story. He'd had a steady girlfriend with cystic fibrosis who died the year before. Jennifer didn't ask if he loved Marie because Jennifer wasn't sure she wanted to hear him say it. But knowing he could feel something deep like that convinced her that, living in a basement or not, she was right where she wanted to be.

His smile came out of nowhere this time. "Your sister told me about you."

Heather had filled Jennifer in on that part. Heather was three years older and ridiculously protective of her clothes and had all kinds of rules about Jennifer not wearing them, but they got along. Heather answered the big questions about boys and make-up.

And she'd mentioned Paul. Jennifer just realized that while Heather was talking about him, she might also be filling him in on Jennifer. It was a scary thought, especially since there hadn't been many details on Paul but Heather had way too much ammo on Jennifer.

"What did she say?" she asked.

"Have I got a girl for you."

She missed something. Jennifer put down the photo of him with a group of boys she recognized but couldn't name and focused on the conversation. "What?"

"That's what Heather said."

"A girl."

"Yeah."

"She was talking about me?"

He moved closer, pushing in close and stopping only when Jennifer's hands brushed against his chest. "Is there a third sister I don't know about?"

Jennifer had never heard him laugh before and it sent her heart tumbling to her feet. "No."

"I like your shirt." He ran his fingers over the ruffle.

Her breath caught. "Why?"

"Because it's pretty . . . like you."

His eyes went to the clock on the wall. "It's almost midnight."

She started the mental countdown. New Year's, it was the perfect time for him to kiss her, and she prayed he would. As the seconds ticked by, a voice in her head screamed for him to do something.

She followed the second hand until it hit twelve. "And now that it's midnight . . .?"

He didn't move, but his sweet smile turned to something else. "Happy New Year's."

She tried to say it back to him, but the words stuck in her throat.

His palms cupped her cheeks.

His warm lips touched against hers, soft and not completely sure. They pressed once and then parted. His eyes opened and he stared down at her.

"Can we do that again?" she whispered the question before she could stop the words from coming out.

"As much as you want."

Her heartbeat hammered in her ears as he lowered his head again and his breath blew across her cheek. "Really?"

A smile tugged at the corner of his mouth. "Really."

Then his mouth was on hers and she forgot about everything else. Her fingers played with the soft hair at the base of his neck. Her breath caught while her body tingled.

Wrapped in his arms, listening to the mix of synthesizer and guitar in the background while his lips moved over hers, she felt free. Her body melted against his and her mind want blank. She wanted only this. The comfort and warmth, the sense of security and acceptance.

She'd known even then this make-out session was just the start, that they'd continue to date and get to know each other. She wasn't too young or confused. This meant something. It was special.

"Paul." Jennifer shoved against his shoulder and struggled to sit up. Being pinned to the backseat of his car with a seatbelt digging into her hip and her skirt shoved up high on her thighs wasn't the problem. She was where she wanted to be. Heck, she picked the location for their kissing session.

What happened if this went one step farther was the issue. The word irreversible floated through her mind.

His mouth sucked on that sweet spot right behind her ear that made her shiver. "You are so beautiful."

She knew she could say the word and he'd stop, but how in the world was she supposed to slam on the brakes to the petting when he kissed her like that? He knew where to touch her.

Then his hand slipped lower and her common sense came rushing back in a flash. She didn't know much about boys, but she guessed they had about five seconds until they strayed into danger territory. "Paul."

"What?" He lifted his head. His eyes were glazed with passion and his finger brushed close to the very center of her.

She almost laughed. Would have if he didn't look so serious and she wasn't right on the verge of giving in. "We talked about this."

He balanced over her on one elbow as his chest rose and fell. "Uh-huh."

"We agreed."

He nodded. "I said I'd wait for you."

"Exactly."

"Right." He blew out a long exhale and dropped his head for a second. His hair tickled her cheek and hot breaths brushed across her skin. "Any idea when that time is going to be?"

She slipped her fingers through his hair as she smiled at his joke. "It's too soon."

"I understand you're worried, but you do know going all the way won't change anything. I'm not going to stop you from doing new things."

"Not on purpose."

His head flew up and his body stiffened. It was as if every muscle screeched to a halt as the frown spread across his mouth. "What is that supposed to mean?"

"I'm not ready." She blurted it out and skipped over the other part, the bigger part. The part where he hid stuff from her.

He'd disappear for a day or two and not get in touch with her. He had started hanging out with two guys who made her nervous. She'd heard the rumors about them. That they'd stopped going to

school and hung out on the streets all day. The idea of Paul with
them made her sick . . . and scared.

"I'm sorry," she whispered.

His smile seemed forced, but he shot her one. "Hey, don't apologize. I want you to be able to tell me anything. Even things like
this that I don't like hearing all that much."

But he wouldn't do the same for her. Sometimes she'd ask questions she knew the answers to, like where he was on a Friday night,
and he wouldn't tell the truth. He kept pretending, and it drove
her nuts, made her want to challenge him even more.

"Okay," she said because she didn't know what else to say.

A smile eased across his lips into something more genuine. "I
can wait. You're worth the sacrifice."

She wasn't buying the complete innocent act. If he could find
a way in . . . he would. "And you're happy as long as we get to do
other stuff."

"Well, yeah. I'm not dead." He kissed her then, his mouth moving over hers as his body pressed her deeper into the cushions.

When he finally lifted his head, her lips felt swollen and her
head spun with a churning excitement that hit her every time she
went into his arms.

"I won't rush you," he said.

But would he ever tell her the truth? "I know."

His hand hovered right above her breast. "But I will keep trying
to change your mind."

"How will you do that?"

He brushed his mouth over hers. "Well, let me show you."

They repeated the scene several times by the end of the school
year and most of the next. Paul would try to push the line and she

would hold firm at the last possible second. Barely.

She had turned sixteen, but they had been inseparable since that first kiss. But it still wasn't enough.

"I like him." Jennifer's grandmother threw out her opinion one afternoon as she watched Paul fix a loose fence post in Jennifer's backyard.

The Duchess and Jennifer sat on the back porch, lemonade in hand, and watched Paul work. Jennifer smiled as warm sun hit her face. "Me too."

"He'll take some work."

The Duchess often said stuff like that. She'd give an opinion no one asked for and then argue her point to death. Never mind if she was the only one arguing. She was a strong presence. The person who taught Jennifer to do everything from write poetry to drink wine. The Duchess viewed life as a never-ending adventure.

"Paul is pretty easygoing," Jennifer said.

The Duchess's eyebrow lifted. "No."

The knowing look sent a ball of nerves bouncing around inside of Jennifer. It was as if her grandmother could glance inside and see the truth. "What?"

"That's not what you like about him."

"Of course it is." Jennifer put her best force behind the words even as she stumbled over the last one.

"You like his darkness. The mystery intrigues you." The Duchess nodded her head as her gaze stayed on Paul. "I don't know a woman alive who can resist a bad boy."

"Grandma!"

The older woman waved her off. "Accept it now."

"He's not bad," Jennifer insisted.

"What is he?"

Jennifer didn't have to search for the word. She'd already figured that much out. "Complicated."

"Exactly." The Duchess nodded. "That's another word for dark,
my dear."

The Duchess's words ran through Jennifer's head a month later,
but she pushed them aside. Maybe Paul didn't share *everything*,
but he was good to her. Understood her. When she talked about
all she wanted to do in the world and how she had to leave home
to do it, he played along.

"We should pick a time in the future for us to get everything
done and then get back together." Jennifer delivered her suggestion as she munched on a handful of chips. "You know, when
we're old."

His knees pressed against hers where they sat next to each
other on the steps outside her father's office. "Give me a number."

"Thirty."

He peeked into the near empty bag before scooping out some
crumbs. "That's a long time from now."

"You need to play your music and get the band started, then
tour." She ticked off his dreams because she knew them as well as
her own.

"True."

"I want to travel and learn everything I can."

"About what?"

She shrugged. "I'm not sure yet."

"Okay. So we agree on thirty."

She loved that he didn't get all twitchy when she talked about
the future. She assumed they'd stay in touch, and so did he. There
was a strange comfort in that.

"But we'll be together between now and then," she said.

"Of course."

She brushed the chip dust off on her skirt and handed him the bag. "Here."

"What's this for?"

"We'll keep this until that day."

He leaned over and treated her to a quick kiss on the lips. "Deal."

"Deal."

Two

*There's a reason your first love is called
your first and not your only.*

—Grandma Gladys, The Duchess

PAUL COULDN'T TAKE ONE MORE SECOND OF HER cross-examination. All he wanted to do was walk her home. The whole ten-thousand-questions, give-me-your-life-story thing was pissing him off. They'd been dating for two years. She should be over this by now.

"Paul?"

He stopped in the middle of the abandoned railroad tracks that ran behind her house and stared at her. They were so close to the yard. So close to her family's kitchen, where they could sit and get something to drink and he wouldn't have to dodge *the talk*.

When she started talking again, he lost it. "Enough."

Jennifer's head snapped back as if he'd slapped her. "What?"

"We've been walking for ten minutes and you haven't stopped screaming at me since." By the way her mouth dropped opened he guessed he'd insulted her. "A guy can only take so much."

He said the last part in a softer tone. He knew from experience getting angry only tipped off her temper. Then they'd fight and

12

break up for a few days. They did it many times, and it ticked him off each one. She'd turn cold and distant, and he'd be the one left out until she agreed to talk to him again. Eventually, they'd get back together, but the cycle got old fast.

He rushed to calm her down. "Can't we just walk?"

She pulled her hand away when he tried to hold it. "How can you say I screamed? I didn't even raise my voice at you."

"That's not the point."

She folded her arms across her chest and gave him that look he hated. The one that reminded him of a scolding teacher. "Where were you today?" she asked.

"Around."

"Not at school."

Looked like she wasn't going to let up, but since he hated all the questions he wasn't going to make it easy for her. "No."

"Why?"

His mind shut off. He tried to come up with an excuse, but nothing popped into his head. His defenses shot up right after. "I didn't feel like it."

"What kind of answer is that?"

"You sound like your father."

"Paul."

"Look, I work. I've always worked. You know that." She didn't know the rest. About why or how much.

"What about school?"

"I prefer work." Even that was a little lie. He worked because he had to and hadn't been enrolled in school all year. He hung around because of her. To see her. To be with her.

"What aren't you sharing?"

"Nothing."

She looked about two seconds away from stomping her foot. "Paul!"

"You and your stupid sharing thing." He mumbled the words under his breath but knew she'd heard him when her eyes grew wide. "Look, it's not that easy."

"I don't know what you're talking about."

He blew out a long breath. His skinned crawled with the sudden need to get out of there, but he ignored the instinct this one time and held his ground. "Years ago, before we met, I went to another school."

"Which one?"

"Not important." Telling her about a home for troubled boys would put that pitying look in her eyes, and he sure didn't want that. "The point is that I was a kid and went on this school camping trip. While in the park, a friend and I got lost. We didn't know we were lost until we were, and by then it was too late. It was one of those 'just a few more feet' things until we were so far from camp and everything looked the same that we had no hope of getting back."

Her arms fell to her sides as she stepped in closer. "What did you do?"

"We yelled for help and circled around. I kept trying to look for something familiar, but I had never been there before and . . . well, every tree looked like every other tree. Nothing stood out."

"What happened?"

"We wandered around for three days."

She grabbed his hands in hers. "What?"

"There was a search, and a helicopter rescue team eventually spotted us."

"Were you hurt?"

He shrugged off the memories of the cold and all those mosquito bites, of being afraid and terrified of showing it. "Nothing serious."

"So what happened?"

"I learned that I have to be smart and fend for myself. That I can't be in a position where I have to depend on help like that again."

Her eyes narrowed.

"What?" he asked.

"That's the wrong lesson."

He shook his head. Only Jennifer would make a declaration like that. "How do you figure?"

"You should have learned that you need people. That sharing things—in that case, where you were—will keep you out of trouble."

He thought about dropping her hands, but she held on tight enough to crush his thumb. "Uh, no."

"Sounds like the right lesson to me."

"You're such a girl."

She smiled. "Thank you for noticing."

He threw an arm around her shoulders and pulled her tight against his side as he started walking. "Oh, I noticed."

Her hand rested on the top of his belt at the small of his back. "I'm sorry you got lost."

"It was a long time ago."

"But still."

He kissed her forehead. "We're all lost sometimes."

She tilted her head back and stared up at him with the sun lighting her face. "That sounds pretty deep."

"But true." He kissed her then, taking his time even as they stumbled over the uneven railroad ties beneath their sneakers.

When he finally lifted his head she continued to stare up at him in that way. The one that made him feel invincible and important.

"Are you lost now?" She whispered the question against his neck.

"Not when I'm with you."

Jennifer sat in her small university apartment and stared at her closed textbooks on the mattress in front of her. Business classes. English classes. She tried to think about anything except the man hovering in her bedroom doorway.

The years had passed. He'd filled out across the shoulders and still wore that sexy smile that made her heart thump until she thought it would pound right out of her chest. Seeing him made her doubts disappear and her judgment cloud.

So much had happened, yet little had changed. He held back information, important information, and then ducked when confronted. They kept moving, but she feared they were racing in different directions. She still wasn't sure where she was going or what she wanted from life, but she was even less sure of him. Not of her feelings but of the world he wanted for himself and how she fit into that.

Paul pushed away from the door frame and stepped into the room. His hands stayed in his back pocket and his jean jacket hung open to show the tee underneath. "How did you find out?"

"Of all the questions you could ask, that's the one you pick?" She threw her pen against the desk and watched it bounce then roll. She didn't even try to stop it when it fell off the edge and hit the floor.

He didn't back down. "Where did you hear it?"

"A friend told me."

He balanced a hand against her desk but didn't move in closer or lean down. "And that's why you're angry. Because you got it through a third party."

She looked at him then. Really looked. Saw the locked jaw and blank stare. For all the maturity he shouldered in working so hard and paying his own way, he remained clueless about simple relationship dynamics. "Do you really not know why?"

Paul shrugged the way he always shrugged when he wanted to avoid a conversation. "It wasn't a big deal."

"You got in trouble and thrown in jail." To anyone else, it would be a tragedy. To Paul, it wasn't even worth mentioning during a dinner date.

"One day. And I'm out." He scoffed. "It's fine."

It was the exact opposite of fine in Jennifer's mind. "It's one more thing."

"What the hell does that mean?"

"You never told me you dropped out of school to work full time. I had to find out about it later, well after the fact."

"It wasn't a big deal."

"Or that you were on your own in that basement all those years ago. That you weren't living with your family." She used her fingers to tick off the list of the facts he never shared and only admitted after she confronted him.

"I've been emancipated since I was fifteen. It's—"

She threw her head back and groaned before staring him down again. "Another 'no big deal' thing, right?"

Clear emotion passed over his face now. Anger. "Why does any of this matter? You think not having the official degree makes me less of a person?"

She pointed at him. "Don't do that. I've never judged you like that."

"Fair enough."

"It's not about what's happened to you. It's about your failure to communicate."

He shook his head. "Women always say that."

"In this case, we're right."

"So what are you trying to tell me?"

The one thing she never wanted to say but kept saying. They'd broken up several times. They'd been apart long enough to date other people before finding their way back to each other again. The scenario stayed the same. And so did their issues.

She was ready to move on and figure out what she wanted from life. He wanted to stay where he was and hide the things he never wanted to say. It was a combination destined for a raging explosion. They needed space before they blew apart, never to come together again.

"We need to see other people." It actually hurt to say the words, as if each one was sliced out of her.

He didn't look any better than she felt. He closed his eyes on a long exhale. "You're doing this again?"

"Tell me what's changed."

"Damn it, Jennifer." He clamped his lips together.

She could almost see him counting to ten. She concentrated on that instead of the ball of anxiety splashing around in her stomach. When he walked out—and she knew from experience he would pick that over fighting to stay—she would crumble. Just fall to the floor in a puddle of tears.

Until then, she sat there with her hands clenched on her lap and tried not to break. Tried not to think about the sharp pains in her head and the stranglehold on her heart.

"You're sure?" he asked.

No. "Yes."

"Here." He reached into his pocket and dropped an envelope on her desk.

"What are these?" By the time she unfolded the flap and looked up he was back at the door. She pulled out a stack of photos. "Paul?"

"I took those when we were at the park last week." He swallowed hard enough for her to see his throat move. "They're yours now."

With numb fingers she flipped through the top few. All photos of her, carefree and smiling. The wind taking her long hair and the laughter fierce enough on the page for her to hear the faint memories of it in her head.

He'd captured the sunshine she felt inside. The moments of pure pleasure.

He saw so much and understood so little.

She slipped to the floor with the photos cradled in her hands. With each one, the tears fell harder. She leaned against the leg of the desk and let the pain wash over her. This time could be the end . . . and the possibility doubled her over.

Three

Be sure before you give up on anything.

—Grandma Gladys, The Duchess

PAUL HADN'T SEEN JENNIFER IN ALMOST TWO YEARS. Finding the old photo of her at the back of his drawer got his mind wandering. He tried hours of hard labor to drive it back out again, but it didn't work. Her image played in his head until he couldn't think of anything else.

He draped one arm over his eyes as he lay on the beat-up plaid couch in his apartment. After all this time, he still saw her face when he closed his eyes. There had been other women, but she wouldn't leave his head.

Distance didn't help either. She was in Toronto. He was almost four hours away in Windsor.

He worked, he played in his band. He lived his life, but still . . .

She'd spent her high-school years breaking up with him, getting back together, and then dumping him again. They tried for a few years after that before drifting apart. Somehow more than seven years had passed and everything they promised fell away. It was as if they never meant anything to each other.

She had been so rigid, wouldn't listen to his side or let him explain in his own time and in his own way. Sure, he'd made mistakes and ran with a crowd that made her nervous, but he handled it, and she should have known it would be okay. Maybe he he hadn't told her everything, but how did a guy tell his girl that he was out of the house and bouncing around on his own before hitting high school?

When you didn't have anything, you had to do some questionable things to earn money, to survive. But Jennifer, with her close family and warm house, would never understand that. His life was so outside her experience. She was so perfect and untouched, and he'd been desperate not to suck her into his world.

And she threw him away.

Even as his brain built a wall against her, his body ached. She was so beautiful, with wide hazel eyes and a smoking body that drove him wild. The shoulder-length brown curls from high school had grown longer, straighter and darker the last time he saw her. The glowing smile, the hitch in her voice when he touched her—the memory of it all drove him wild.

He clenched his hand into a fist against his thigh and tried not to think about her and everything that had gone wrong. His head buzzed with the loss.

After a few seconds, his eyes popped open and he glanced around the room. The buzz came from outside his body. The phone was ringing.

He reached over his head and grabbed it. His greeting came out in a voice raspy with need. "Hey."

"Paul?"

He blinked a few times. *Not possible.*

"Hello?" The uncertainty in her voice came through the line loud and clear.

He shook his head, trying to figure out how his deepest fantasies had sprung to life. "Jennifer? Is that you?"

She blew out a breath. "You remember."

As if he could forget anything about her. Even the smile in her voice sounded the same. "Of course."

"I worried that . . . well, it's not important."

"I was just thinking about you." He blurted it out knowing she would never believe him. He still didn't believe the timing. Her husky laugh vibrated through him. "You were thinking about me. I was thinking about you. How convenient."

"Not the word I'd use, but yeah." He didn't want to question his luck in this moment, but he had to know. "Why are you calling me now?"

She hesitated, and the silence grew.

"Jennifer?"

"I missed you."

The words knocked the breath out of him. "Me too," he rushed out once he regained his voice.

"I wasn't sure you'd want to hear from me. Because of how it ended."

He bit back the words "Which time?" and went with something more neutral. Now that she had made a move and he had her talking, he wasn't about to mess it up. "You were furious."

"You lied to me."

A familiar tension built in his gut. He clenched his jaw and mentally beat it back. "I didn't tell you everything."

"It's the same thing."

He refused to argue with her. Instead, he sighed, conceding this round to her. "I learned my lesson. Trust me."

Losing her—again and again—had cost him something. As hard

as he tried to wipe her from his head and move on, he was only going through the motions. He missed her like hell. Wanted her. Needed to see her, hear her laugh, watch her face as her mind ran in different directions and she rushed to get the words out.

He loved that about her. The fiery excitement with which she met every challenge. Every challenge but him.

But he didn't want to rehash. Definitely didn't want to run through the details on his rough home life or finally explain the stint in jail for a dumb prank.

He needed her voice to wash over him so he could pretend she was right there beside him. "I still can't believe the timing."

"You really were thinking about me? That wasn't just a line?"

"It's true."

"I can't explain it." She fumbled around with a few words before she got the sentence out. "You've been on my mind more and more. Then Heather mentioned seeing a friend of yours and I finally gave into the urge and called."

"I'm happy you did."

"You sound it."

The comfortable banter came winging back as if they'd never lost it. "And you still have the sexiest voice I've ever heard."

"It's just a regular voice."

"Wrong."

She laughed. "You sure you weren't doing something more than thinking when I called?"

When her voice dipped low like that, the blood pounded in his groin. "You always were a smart woman."

"Yeah, that's what I thought." Something rustled in the background, then her voice came through even clearer. "So, what am I wearing during all of this thinking you're doing?"

He let his hand move closer to his zipper. "Nothing."

"Interesting."

This was his Jennifer. He could share the most intimate details of his body with her without embarrassment. She would know from the way he'd lose his breath what just hearing her was doing to his lower half.

"Actually, that's not quite right," he admitted.

"Lingerie? Panties?"

"Me." He unbuckled his pants.

"Very nice."

"And hearing you now—"

"Let's see what happens if I keep talking."

"We've talked on the phone every day." Jennifer wrapped the telephone cord around her index finger as she talked. Perched on the edge of her bed in her shorts pajamas, all of her concentration centered on the call. On the subtle changes in Paul's deep voice as he talked.

"Is that bad?"

"No, but I thought I'd mention it." She hoped he'd get he hint, jump in his car and get to her. The four hours that separated them stretched even wider the longer they limited their contact to the phone.

"Uh-huh."

She'd heard that noncommittal boy-talk before. Didn't care for it all that much. "And that means?"

"I don't claim to know much about women, but since you *mentioned* the frequency of our calls, I'm wondering if you were trying to tell me something." Amusement filled his voice, hinting that he knew exactly what she was saying.

If he wanted her to beg, he'd have to keep on waiting. "Just throwing it out there."

"Uh-huh."

"Is that your new favorite phrase?"

"For the record, you can pretty much say anything and I'll be a fan of it."

He always did know how to make her smile. "Sweet talker."

"I'm getting a lot of practice."

She tightened her hold on the phone as she fell back against her mattress. "Now who's harping on the frequency of our calls?"

"Still you."

She stretched her arm over her head and closed her eyes, letting the sound of his voice wash over her. "We could do something about it, you know?"

"What's 'it'?"

"I'm rolling my eyes at you." She actually kept them closed, but he didn't have to know that.

"That's a very sexy look on you."

"You can only imagine."

He laughed. "I'm just seeing how long it takes you to crack and say what you're trying not to say."

Challenge accepted. "Oh, you underestimate me. I can hold out longer than you can."

"Apparently, because these calls are killing me."

She considered that close enough to a win to skip ahead. "We could . . . you know."

"Actually see each other?"

"A radical idea, I know."

"Certainly raises some interesting possibilities."

She imagined him wiggling his eyebrows and doing all sorts

of naughty things with his hand. "We've been handling that over the phone."

"Keep talking like that and we will again."

She couldn't help but smile at that one. "Before we get side-tracked, what about it, and if you ask me what 'it' is I will smack you."

"Maybe I'll surprise you by landing on your doorstep." His voice dropped to a new level of husky.

"I'll be counting the days until you do."

Four

Surprises tend to be better for the giver than the receiver.

—Grandma Gladys, The Duchess

JENNIFER COULDN'T BELIEVE MORE THAN A MONTH passed since Paul's initial call without him showing up on her doorstep. He knew where she lived because she'd told him. They talked all the time since that out-of-nowhere call that had him panting into the phone and her needing to see him again. Wondering what the adult version of that handsome face looked like and who he turned out to be was killing her.

She'd moved into an apartment with Heather and her boyfriend, Ted. All those years of tagging along as the baby sister had become a habit. Jennifer enjoyed spending time with Heather, talking about men and life, and Ted was a good guy. Good to Heather.

But tonight Jennifer sat in the middle of the overstuffed beige sofa with a stack of fashion magazines at her side and a glass of wine in her hand, and she listened to the silence. She wore the slim jeans that showed off her butt and the loose purple tee that looked so good against her pale skin. She dressed with a purpose. For company.

Ted had hustled Heather out of the apartment with a hastily packed overnight bag and a vague promise of the perfect camping destination. Jennifer knew what that meant: Paul finally was on his way.

Ted knew Paul from Sarnia. They'd all grown up in the same area. The inevitable chain of events where Jennifer told Heather about the call, and Ted called Paul, had occurred. Jennifer knew it would, which was why she only gave Heather some of the details about the telephone conversation.

But no one bothered to fill Jennifer in on this evening's plans. They didn't have to. Her awareness of Paul had never wavered. In some sense she could feel him and track his movements, knowing there was more for them.

The doorbell rang right as she finished her drink. Her insides raced, begging her to run to the door and drag him inside. The only thing that stopped her was her grandmother's voice in her head, telling her not to make it too easy.

She threw the door open anyway. Even stopped by the mirror in the entry to make sure her hair wasn't sticking out in ten different directions first.

Paul smiled the instant he saw her. "Hey."

He stood there, his tawny hair only a few inches off his shoulders. And what great shoulders they were, broad and falling to a trim waist. The faded blue jeans and white button-down shirt showed off the muscles he'd developed while they were apart. Whatever he had been doing for the last few years included a lot of activity because she couldn't see an inch of fat on him.

"Paul."

"You weren't expecting someone else?"

"Just you."

"How are you?" She wanted to say so much, but only a lame bit of nonsense came out.

"At the moment?" His gaze did a quick tour of her face. "Pretty damn good."

Her hand tightened on the side of the door where she leaned against it. "I was hoping you'd finally come here."

Heat rushed to her cheeks. She knew without looking she was blushing, and not from embarrassment. No, it came from the excitement ramping up inside of her. From the realization that all those years later, Paul still had the power to make her stomach flip flop and her knees turn to mush.

"Jennifer?"

"Yeah."

His eyebrow lifted. "Any chance I can come inside?"

She waved her hand in front of her face. "Of course."

For her, the question had really always been whether she'd ever be able to let him leave if she needed room. Seeing him now brought back a rush of desire and longing. The want mixed with the deep sense of coming home.

She pushed it all out of her mind and tried to concentrate on the now. "It just so happens I'm alone this weekend."

He shot her one of those sexy you're-all-mine grins she remembered so well. "Now, isn't that convenient?"

"I'm sure you didn't have anything to do with Ted and Heather disappearing for a few days."

"I'd love to talk about that . . ." Paul leaned in, throwing a quick glance at her death grip on the door. "If you'll let me come inside."

What was wrong with her? She shook her head and stepped back. "Sorry."

"You're not alone. I feel it, too."

"What?"

He slid inside and closed the door behind him. "It's like I'm ten seconds away from breaking into a million pieces."

He understood. "But yet I'm not afraid," she said.

"Didn't think you were."

"I'm not sure what's happening or why I'm acting like I've lost my mind." She wasn't sure she liked the vulnerable feeling either, but she didn't fight it for now.

He crowded in, bringing his head close enough for their noses to touch. "If I don't kiss you soon, my head will explode."

Like that, she stopped shifting her weight from foot to foot and the awkwardness fled. "Well, we can't have that."

"Thank God." He closed the few inches separating them.

She threw her arms around his shoulders and plunged her fingers through his hair. The utter rightness of holding him flooded through her. He smelled like the woods after a rain.

The years passed into nothing and all that mattered was the feel of his strong hands on her back and his chest pressing against her breasts. When his mouth covered hers, all resistance melted. Lips slanted and taunted. His tongue dipped inside, and the kiss pulled even deeper.

After a few minutes of hot mouths and wandering hands, he raised his head. "That's quite a greeting."

"The Duchess trained me to be a good host."

"Always liked your grandmother."

"She told me you were dashing."

His smile grew impossibly wide. "I get that all the time. All the grandmothers think I'm hot."

"I'm not responding to that."

"Good call."

Jennifer's fingertips traced the outline of his mouth as he joked. "It took you long enough to get here."

"I had to finalize some things."

"You hang up a phone, you grab a toothbrush and get in your car. How hard is that?" She tried to keep her tone light even though it ticked her off that he could stay away after all those calls. She hadn't shared the same sense of restraint.

"There was a bit more to my plans than that."

"Why?"

"Not to be rude, but do you really want to talk right now?"

She could feel him press against her stomach. At five-nine, she was only a few inches shorter and they fit together so well. "You poor thing."

"I've waited a long time to get you alone, in a bed . . ." He rubbed his hands up and down her arms. "Do you need me to be more specific about where my mind is going?"

"I thought we'd sit down, have some coffee and talk."

His face turned an odd shade of green. "I . . . uh . . ."

She could actually see his eyes widen. He clearly was too far gone to pick up the sarcasm. "Paul, I'm kidding."

"Well, I mean, I can tolerate some talking if you want."

"About what?"

"I have no idea."

"The talking has been going well for you for the last month."

The sickly green around his mouth faded a bit. "Have I thanked you for that?"

"Yes."

He blew out a long breath and wiped a hand through his hair. "Look, it's not that I don't want to talk—"

"It's okay. You can stop fumbling around now. I don't want mindless chit-chat either."

He threw his head back. "Thank you!"

"Though it was pretty cute to watch you panic."

"I was trying not to sound like a jerk on a booty call."

"You're coming across more like a guy who is inches away from getting something he wants."

He glanced down. "Inches. Yeah, that's one way to look at it."

She toyed with the idea of torturing him a bit longer, but since she wanted him as much as he wanted her, she abandoned the thought. This wasn't a test. If it were, he'd already passed long ago.

She slipped her hand in his and stepped back until there was enough room for air to move between them again. "I think we should start with a tour of the house."

His shoulders fell. "Jennifer . . ."

"Yeah?"

"You're killing me here."

"We'll start with my bedroom."

The bleak tension left his face. "That sounds perfect."

Paul tried to take in the details of her bedroom. He dreamed about what her most private sanctuary would look like, what she would keep and throw away. But it was all a blur. She could have had the walls painted black with hockey masks hanging from the ceiling and he never would have known. His eyes were for her only.

The press of her palm against his brought back memories of walking down the hallway at school. Seeing her butt swish from side to side made him remember how she used to love skirts and how much he enjoyed getting his hands underneath them.

Not that he didn't appreciate the jeans. She filled them out just fine. They hugged every curve and highlighted her long legs. But he longed to get her out of them. He was desperate for her. Like, put-your-life-on-hold-crazy-to-be-with-her desperate.

She guided him past a small desk to the double bed in the center of the room. He saw stacks of pillows and a white comforter.

Then he only saw her. She moved in front of him, her dark hair falling over her shoulders and eyes flushing from hazel to a bright green, as they always did when she was aroused.

"You are still the most beautiful woman I've ever seen." He'd measured every date by her and found the others lacking.

"And you still make me weak when you smile."

"Good thing there's a bed behind you." He eased her down until they sat next to each other on the mattress with legs touching.

A wave of uncertainty washed over him. He knew how to pleasure and entice women, but this was Jennifer. She was special. He wanted it to be right and perfect. They had waited so long to come together, he didn't want to blow it now.

"What are you thinking?" She leaned against his shoulder with her head tucked under his neck and her hand on his stomach.

That she could do better than him. The fact she even gave him a chance continued to shock him. "We're wearing too many clothes."

"Subtle." She lifted her head and kissed him on the chin.

"Believe me, I'm showing remarkable restraint."

"And why is that exactly?"

He didn't miss the teasing in her voice or the husky invitation behind it. "Good question. Guess I'm slow."

"Never that."

"Well, I'm about to fix the mistake."

He kissed her, letting his mouth wander over every inch of her lips before pressing long and deep. It was a kiss filled with pent-up heat and desire. He didn't hold back or try to play games. He let her feel every lonely moment.

When they broke apart, she was flat against the bed with him looming over her. Her arms tugged on his hair and pulled him down for a second round of mind-blowing kisses.

His control broke.

Fingers found the edge of her T-shirt and pushed it up. She lifted her shoulders and helped him strip it off. His lips found the tops of her breasts where they plumped over her bra as her hands snaked up his back.

She froze. "Wait."

"What?"

"Stop."

Not again. "Damn it, Jennifer."

"It's not what you think."

"We're grown-ups this time. We don't have to wait or sneak around."

"Not that." She shoved his shirt up to his neck and sat up to peek around him. "What's on your back."

He felt what blood he had remaining in his brain leave his head with a loud whoosh. "Oh."

"You got *another* tattoo?" She sounded distressed about the discovery.

He knew why. She hated tattoos. She made that quite clear when he got the first one at sixteen. She'd gone on and on about how he ruined his smooth back and how his body had been perfect without any marks.

He hadn't really known what ticked her off so badly. He wanted one and got it. Simple. It was a step toward independence and leaving a rough childhood behind, and he'd never regretted it. No matter how much she'd bitched.

"I could lie, but since you can see it, I'll go with yes." He swallowed, worried he'd somehow blown it again. "It's a tattoo."

"That's all you've got to say?"

"It's been years." He knew he should stop talking, but she raised his defenses and he wasn't ready to bring them back down again. "You weren't there when I made the decision."

She opened her mouth and then closed it again before saying anything. "True."

"Okay." Several beats of silence passed before he ventured back to the dangerous topic. "Is the fight over?"

"Yes."

He wasn't exactly sure what just happened, but he seemed to have won, or at least he didn't lose. "That would be more convincing if you weren't frowning at me."

The flat line of her mouth curled up at one end. "I sometimes forget that we've been apart."

"But we're here now." He slid his hand over her knee. "Together."

The stiffness left her shoulders as she fell back against the bed. "Where we want to be."

"That was my observation, too." He took his shirt the rest of the way off and threw it on the floor.

"Did I kill the mood?" She chuckled as she said it, her nervousness obvious.

"Hardly."

"I just—"

He put his finger over her lips. "You could stand on a corner wearing a garbage bag and screaming obscenities at me and I'd still want you."

"Still such the sweet talker."

"It's the truth."

She trailed her hand down his bare chest to the top of his belt. "Is there anything I can do to get us back where we were before I had my fit?"

"Let me think." He rolled on top of her and groaned at the feel of his body against hers.

"You don't need this." She unhooked the belt and slipped it out of his pants.

"I could say the same about you." He popped the button loose on the top of her jeans.

Her body trembled when the back of his hand brushed against her bare skin of her stomach. He enjoyed the sensation so much, he did it a second time and felt her sharp intake of breath against his hair.

The press of her hand against his fly and steady thud of her heart against his broke the last of her control reserves.

He sat back and stripped her slim jeans down her legs, taking her panties as he went. When she was naked, with her body flushed and him kneeling between her legs, he took a long, agonizing look at her. He had caressed that skin many times as a fumbling teenager. Now he was coming to her as a man.

He pressed forward, trapping her body between his elbows, and lowered his chest against hers. His muscles shook with the force of holding himself back as he pressed a trail of kisses along her jawline.

Her back arched off the bed. "Paul . . . now."

"Yes, now."

Five

⌒

Sex doesn't always mean the same thing for men
as it does for women. But sometimes it does.

—Grandma Gladys, The Duchess

AFTER YEARS OF WAITING AND FOUR ROUNDS OF
lovemaking, Paul could barely speak. He hoped the apartment
didn't catch on fire because he'd never be able to get off the
bed and rescue them. They'd been back together for only a few
hours and he couldn't move . . . couldn't imagine another day
without her.

He lifted his head and glanced around her room. With the sun
streaming in the window and his need for her satisfied at least
temporarily, he could see the place much better. Everything was
white and blue and very feminine. The citrus scent he associated
with her filled the room. There were clothes and books stacked
everywhere.

The controlled chaos reflected Jennifer. She was a thundering
ball of energy. She stormed in and out of his life and left him
breathless with each turn. No matter how harsh the words that
passed between them, he couldn't hold onto the anger. She was
smart and so sexy it hurt to look at her.

Even now she lay sprawled over half the bed, which was impressive since she didn't weigh all that much and sure didn't take up much room despite her height. Since he'd kissed and caressed every inch of her the night before, he could describe her without opening his eyes.

But what a joy it was to open them and look at her.

They'd wrecked the bed. There was a sheet waded up underneath his shoulder and pillows spread across the floor. Her panties hung on the lampshade, and his jeans were thrown on a pile on the floor of her open closet. He had no idea how either piece of clothing got to their final resting places.

Just when he decided to roll her over and wake her up the fun way, her bare foot slid up his calf and her arm tightened across his stomach.

"I'm hungry," she mumbled against his skin.

"I thought you were asleep."

She popped up with her head balanced on top of her hands. Her eyes focused solely on him. "Not anymore."

He'd never seen anyone shift from sleep to awake that fast. "It's still early."

"I get up early." She drummed her fingers on his chest. "And I could eat."

"Oh, really?"

"I mean food."

"Oh. Well, don't look at me. I can't move." He doubted he could make his way to the kitchen for a snack. God knew he needed one. A man could only engage in so much sex before the requirement of refueling arose.

"That's not very chivalrous." Her bare leg swung around in a lazy pattern behind her.

From this position he could see straight down her body. He mentally removed the flimsy sheet that was half thrown over her backside. "You sucked the life out of me."

"You seemed pretty happy with my sucking a few hours ago."

"Most definitely."

"So the least you can do is feed me."

He raised his hands in mock surrender. "I give up. You win."

"Good man."

He shifted underneath her, trying to ignore the spark of life to his lower half when her body brushed over his. "Anything to make you happy."

He got the whole way to the kitchen before he realized she had followed him. He opened the refrigerator and turned around to find her leaning against the door frame, wrapped in a wrinkled white sheet.

"What are you doing up?" he asked.

"I missed you."

"Keep saying stuff like that and we'll see how sturdy this table is." He knocked against the wood to emphasize his point.

"You're naked."

"And I plan on staying that way." He grabbed the eggs and a chunk of cheese and dumped them on the counter. "As far as I'm concerned, this is just a break from the action."

"Were you this hot and ready in high school?"

"And every damn day since then."

She stepped into the room, her bare feet slapping against the wood floor. "If we keep up this pace we won't be able to walk by Monday."

"That's the plan." He faced the cabinets and started searching for a pan.

When he stood back up, she was right behind him. She slipped her arms around his waist and pulled tight against him. "I still think waiting was the right thing all those years ago."

He turned around and leaned back against the sink. He guided her to stand between his legs and held her steady with his hands on her hips. "I'm guessing I wasn't a very good risk back then."

"You were sexy and sweet but so mysterious."

"I scared you."

"You once showed up at my parents' house drunk."

He winced over that one. "Admittedly not my finest moment. I was an idiot, but in my defense I was also a horny teen boy."

"I didn't know how to handle you."

"I remember sitting outside your house and hearing you tell your mother you were dumping me." The memory still stung.

Jennifer's eyes widened. "What?"

"You said I'd started hanging around with a dangerous crowd. That I was immature and hiding things from you." He looked away from her so he didn't have to see the sadness in her eyes. He didn't want her pity. He wanted her to understand. "I didn't have anywhere to go, so I just sat there."

"I'm sor—"

"Don't pity me." He shook his head. "I don't want that."

"You were on your own by then and didn't tell me."

"I'm not alone now."

"Paul—"

"I'm with you." He tugged at the sheet tucked over her breasts and let it fall to her feet.

"What are you doing?"

He dropped down in front of her with his knees on the cold floor and her body spread out like a naked feast in front of him.

He slid his hands up the inside of her thighs, opening her legs as he went.

"Are you still confused about what I want?"

She braced her hands on his shoulders. "I'm catching up."

"I've always admired your intelligence."

She pushed his head closer to her body. "Stop talking."

Jennifer tried to remember when she'd felt this free. This alive and happy. Talking to Paul was one thing. Curling up against him in the middle of her bed while he pretended to read sections of the paper to her was something she'd never imagined.

When he finished one story, she pointed to another headline and let him scan the article so he could make up something to go along with the bold letters.

He shook his head and threw her a mock serious look. "You won't be interested in that one."

"Why?"

"There's a dancing frog, a traffic accident and a problem with a school cafeteria. Very nasty stuff."

"The headline says: 'Superintendent in Trouble.'"

"Well, sure. The frog belonged to him."

She laid her hand against Paul's stomach and felt the muscles twitch beneath her fingers. "Even a week ago, would you have thought this possible?"

"Only in my fantasies."

Her heart did a quick jig. "It's pretty sweet having a role in those."

"Nice try at being humble, but you have to know you're the star."

"Since when?"

He pulled back so he could look down at her. "Always."

Since he suddenly seemed so serious, she traced her finger over his full lips. "Have I told you how happy I am you came here?"

"No more than I am that I finally got in that car."

"Took you long enough."

He stared at the ceiling and shook his head with an impressive woe-is-me frown. "Always complaining."

She slid her body over his and drew his attention back with the simple touch of her palm against his cheek. "Have any other ideas of what we can do?"

"I'm only human, you know."

She understood his point. Her happily exhausted body might not even be able to react without a refueling and a bit of rest. "We could cuddle."

He snorted. "I'm betting that lasts for about five minutes."

"Don't think I can control myself?"

He threw the paper over the side of the bed. "I know I can't."

Six

Do not lose your head over a pretty face.

—Grandma Gladys, The Duchess

HEATHER STOOD BY THE SINK ON TUESDAY MORNING. She stopped pouring coffee long enough to look up and smile. "I'm surprised you can still move."

Jennifer inhaled the fresh scent as she dropped into the nearest chair, craving caffeine. "You'll notice I'm sitting."

"So," Heather sat across from her sister and passed a mug in her general direction. "How was it?"

Jennifer ached all over, but in a good way. There wasn't an inch of flesh Paul hadn't conquered. He kissed her until her ankles dug into the mattress and she begged for more. When he pressed inside her, she questioned why she ever made them wait so long.

But there was only so much she was willing to share. She and Heather had traded stories about boys and later men, whispered gossip about everyone they knew, and divulged their most secret wishes. Jennifer cried in Heather's arms after she broke up with Paul years ago.

Despite Heather knowing everything, Jennifer wanted to keep some parts of the intimate weekend private. "A lady doesn't kiss and tell."

43

Heather tapped her fingernails against the table. "She does if she doesn't want her big sister to smack her."

"Seeing him again . . ." Jennifer shook her head, afraid to say anything more and jinx it. "I can't even describe it."

"Try."

"In a word." Jennifer sipped on her coffee and peeked over the rim at her sister. "Fantastic."

"Ha!" Heather sat back with her patented I-told-you-so smile full on her lips. "Aren't you glad you called?"

"You're just trying to take credit."

"I am the one who told you to do it."

"You did not."

"Okay, you were going to do it anyway, but I told you that you should." Heather waved her hand in dismissal. "So, how fantastic? Like off-the-charts or just-getting-started fantastic?"

Paul slipped into the room and leaned against the doorway. "What are we talking about?"

Jennifer didn't know where he found the navy sweatpants and slim gray tee, but she liked the casual look. The relaxed, mussed-from-sleep hair and sexy eyes. It was all she could do not to drag him down the hall to the bedroom one more time.

From the stupid grin on his face, she knew he'd overheard most of the conversation, so she didn't try to hide it. "How amazing you are in bed."

He pushed off from the wall and headed her way. "Well, a man can't ask for more than that."

She lifted her head for a lingering morning kiss. She could feel the smile on his lips and enjoyed the sure hold of his fingers on the back of her neck.

"I admire your humbleness." She mumbled the words against his mouth.

"Handsome and humble. That's quite a combination," Heather said as she reached behind her, letting her chair rest on the back two legs. She swiped another mug off the counter and let it clang against the table.

"I'm impressed you remembered to put pants on." Jennifer tapped his nose before pointing at the chair next to hers.

"I have a few brain cells left, but they're fighting each other for a caffeine fix." The chair let out a loud screech as he dragged it closer to hers and slipped his arms around her shoulders.

"I'm sure your boss will appreciate that." It was the unspoken issue. The one she'd ignored but knew would creep up and smack her eventually. Reality had a way of doing that.

He had a life hours away from hers. She had finished college and was waiting for her marketing job to start. She could afford a few days of fun, but he didn't have that luxury. He had to be self-reliant and responsible all the time, since he was a teenager.

She had Heather to pick up the slack if she needed it. He had no one.

"Thanks for the caffeine reinforcement." He winked at Heather while he said it.

It was what he didn't say that worried Jennifer. He'd ignored her comment and didn't show any signs of coming back to it later. They'd been so busy working out the desire she stockpiled for years, so wrapped up in their intimacy and getting to know each other again, that they'd skipped over the simple details.

"Why aren't you at work?" she asked, trying a second time to get an answer to the question that refused to leave her brain.

"What do you mean?"

"Won't your boss be upset?"

Paul took a long drink. "No."

The pulling-teeth thing made her want to scream. And not in a good way. It reminded her of all the things that ticked her off in the past. "Because?"

"Because I don't have one."

The words splashed against her with the force of a bucket of ice water. Gone was the bantering byplay. This was something she could not joke around or ignore. "What did you say?"

"You heard me."

"Repeat it, and try explaining this time."

"I left my job to come here."

The comment didn't make any sense. It was irresponsible to walk away from a paying job for sex, no matter how long it had been or how good it was. "You quit your job to visit me for the weekend?"

He grabbed the milk and started to pour. "Not really."

She grabbed the pitcher from his hand and thumped it against the table with such force she was surprised it didn't crumble in her hand. "Paul."

"What are you—"

"Talk."

He stared at her for a few seconds too long. "I'm moving here."

"Where?"

"Toronto. More specifically, this apartment." His eyes narrowed. "I thought you figured that out already."

She pushed her chair back and stood up. He couldn't touch her. Not now. She needed a Paul-free-zone and zero temptation to get through this. She refused to be sidetracked by the confusion in those intense green eyes.

She put a chair and the table between them and held the back of her seat in a death grip. "Since when?"

"We talked about this on the phone."

"No. We talked about you coming here for a visit."

"I was talking about relocating."

She tightened her hold. "Did you think to mention it to me?"

"I thought that's what we were doing. Discussing and agreeing."

"Absolutely not."

"I should leave." Heather started to stand up.

Jennifer pointed at the chair her sister had just abandoned. "Sit."

"Okay." Heather's eyes were as wide as Paul's. She sat there, unmoving except for her gaze, which kept switching between Jennifer and Paul.

"Did you know about this?" Jennifer asked Heather, even though she knew the answer.

"Ted mentioned—"

That was all Jennifer needed to know. She held up her hand to Heather and turned her wrath on Paul. "Explain why I'm the last one to get the memo on this event."

"Can you calm down first?"

"No." She seethed. It was a miracle that fire didn't shoot out of the top of her head. "Start."

Paul inhaled as he set his mug away from him and folded his hands together on the tabletop. "Ted and I talked. He said I could come live with you guys and gave me a lead or two on some jobs."

"You're unemployed."

Paul's jaw tightened, but his voice remained even. "I do seasonal construction work. You know that."

"How do you get from there to moving in together?"

"I just thought—"

"What?" she barked at him, unable to control her temper as it raged like an out-of-control beast.

"I can work from here."

This time when Heather stood up Jennifer didn't say anything. With her face pale and her hand shaking, Heather slipped out the door. Jennifer couldn't figure out if she was angry or relieved at not having an audience.

She did have to calm her racing heart or it would beat right out of her chest. She took a deep breath and tried to lower her voice. "You assumed we'd pick up where we left off in high school."

"No, since we didn't live together in high school and we're going to now."

"No, we're not." The harsh whisper sounded so strange in her ears.

"What is wrong with you?"

He wanted to jump over all the hard parts, as if they didn't have a history, when from what she could see his communication skills still needed a lot of work. "You don't get to use an easy pass and step right back into my life without even consulting me."

His mouth dropped open. "You called me."

"I didn't invite you to take half my closet."

He slumped back in his seat with his mouth dropped open. "I have no idea what you're talking about."

He kept pushing her. She felt pressured and backed into a corner. Not that she didn't want to be with him. She did. But she wanted him to work at it, for them to find their way together. She wanted them to go through the natural steps of dating and not fast forward simply because they had a history and were looking for easy.

"We are not living together." She had vowed never to live with a man and was not ready to make an exception after a few great hours together.

"Why?" He out-shouted her with his simple question.

"That's a huge step, and we're not ready."

He growled. Actually threw his head back and let out a loud groan that wound to a yell. When he sat back up, his eyes were alive with fire. "I swear that's your favorite phrase. You throw it out whenever things get a little close between us, then you hide behind it."

"That's not fair."

He threw his arms open wide. "And this is?"

She beat back the unwanted guilt and focused on staying strong. "We're talking."

"You're kicking me out."

"When did I say that?"

"What else do you call it?"

"You're purposely misunderstanding what I'm saying."

"I let my apartment go. I moved here to be with you." He shook his head. "Why in the hell do you think it took me so long to get here after you called the first time?"

That part now made some sense, but his failure to actually state his plans during any of their phone conversations that lonely month made her wonder if he was once again trying to hide something from her. She'd been there and had no interest in going back to the days of trying to engage in mind-reading just to figure out where he had been the night before.

Sure, he was an adult, and according to their mutual friends a pretty responsible one, but he hedged and her defenses went up. She dug in, could feel every muscle in her body tense as her mind spun with worst-case scenarios. She hated that she went there, right to the bad stuff, but the memories were so sharp. She couldn't shake them. And until she could, they needed to back up and go slow.

"You can't make plans without my input, Paul." Her nails dug into the wooden chair. "You're trying to change everything and sweep me right along with you."

"I just want to be with you."

Her resolved softened. "I feel the same."

He shoved the coffee mug away from him. "You're not acting like it."

His anger kept hers brewing. "You . . . you barged in here."

His eyes bugged. "Barged?"

The conversation kept spinning and expanding until it took on an energy all its own. Accusations had to be next. They could circle back around and keep arguing or she could end it.

"You have to leave."

"The house or your life?"

The idea of losing him forever this time slammed into her gut and made her stumble back. "I'm talking about not moving in together."

"Are you sure that's all you're saying, because it sounds deeper to me."

"I'm not talking to you until you move out." She didn't know how else to get his attention but to draw a line and refuse to cross it.

"What kind of crazy childish bullshit is that?"

"You'll live in your house. I'll live in mine. We'll date like normal people."

He wiped a hand through his hair, then stared at her. "You have to be kidding."

"That way we can decide where we are and what we need."

And she hoped with everything inside her they'd discover they needed each other. She'd always felt it there, rumbling in the back of her mind. She wanted a chance to investigate it. Make sure there was something worth nurturing and growing.

A nerve in his cheek twitched. "I know what I want. I don't need to live ten minutes away to figure that out."

"I do."

He threw up his hands. "Of course you do. Why am I surprised?"

A deathly silence descended on the kitchen. Except for the hum of the refrigerator, nothing in the room moved or made a sound. Inside, the blood thundered through her veins and pounded in her ears.

"You're rushing me," she whispered when she couldn't take the quiet one more second.

"Not anymore." Without looking at her, he stood up and walked out of the kitchen.

Ten minutes later, Jennifer stood in the kitchen alone and stunned. The sun rose and burned through the window, but she didn't feel the heat. A deep chill ran through her bones.

"That went well," Heather said in a soft voice as she wrapped an arm around her sister's shoulders and pulled her into a bear hug.

"How dare he—"

Heather broke in. "Think that three nonstop days of sex and talking and feeling great meant something?" The question didn't carry any judgment.

Jennifer needed Heather to understand. Someone had to be on her side in this. "He just walked back into my life. I need a little time to discover what that means before we start making claims on each other and sharing a bathroom. It's too much too fast."

Heather helped Jennifer into the chair and then crouched down beside her. "You did call him in the first place. Wasn't that to rekindle?"

"It was to reconnect. I didn't tell him to move in."

"True." Heather pressed her warm hands against Jennifer's icy ones. "Look, I'm sorry about my part in all of this. Ted jumped too fast, and I got caught up in it. I like you and Paul together. Always have."

Something in her voice grabbed Jennifer's attention. For the first time since Paul walked out, she stared at something besides the broken clock on the far wall. "You knew the whole time?"

"Ted told me on Saturday about the moving plans. I thought it was a good thing because I know how much you care about Paul, how he's never far from your thoughts. But if I had reasoned it through I would have realized it was the wrong move, just too soon, and called to warn you."

"It just feels like a cheat."

"How?"

"Like he's skipping through the tough stuff and pretending we don't have a history or five thousand problems to wade through."

"Okay." Heather blew out a long breath. "I can understand that. So will he if you give him some time. Maybe don't come down so hard."

Jennifer's eyes filled and her throat closed. "I don't want to lose him."

"I know, honey."

"But I don't want him to . . ." She replayed every minute of every weekend conversation in her head, checking for a comment or thread that would lead Paul to think they were jumping to the moving in stage. She found none. "What if he hasn't grown up yet? What if this is the wrong time? We could really blow it forever if we get the timing wrong again."

"Maybe you should forget the no-talk thing and explain all of that to him." Heather squeezed Jennifer's hand, then slid into another chair.

"I just wish he could figure it out without me telling him." That would be the ultimate sign that they'd grown up.

Heather snorted. "Last I checked Paul was still a man."

"Meaning?"

"When you let him into your bed he assumed he had some rights. For him, that was the conversation, and you were saying the same thing."

Jennifer wanted to debate, but Heather was right. The world worked a certain way. By calling him, by dragging him into her bedroom and not letting him out, she'd sent a message. Not the one she meant to deliver, but the one he wanted to hear. And when he acted on it, she lost it.

"The Y chromosome is a dangerous thing," Jennifer mumbled.

"But it does have its benefits."

She remembered the perfect moments before the morning broke apart. "Can't argue with that."

When the front door opened and in from the cold came Heather, Jennifer, and her best friend Tracie, Ted glanced up from his seat on the couch. "Welcome to the armed camp."

"Shut up." Paul's growl of warning was low; his gaze never strayed from the television. He didn't want to talk or joke. He certainly didn't want to rehash the get-lost scene in front of Jennifer's friend. Tracie was nice enough and close with the group, but it was none of her business.

He'd spent three weeks trying to change Jennifer's mind and break through the wall of stubbornness she erected around her, but she refused to budge on her move-out ultimatum. He finally gave in and went apartment and job hunting. Yet he couldn't bring himself to venture outside of Toronto and away from her.

Despite the rage that rumbled in his gut every time she passed him on the way to the bathroom or sat across from him at the breakfast table, he held out hope. She insisted they would start a normal relationship—whatever that was—as soon as he had his own place. He had no idea what geography had to do with seeing each other, but the idea was stuck in her head, which meant he was stuck with following through.

Ted threw their friend Tracie a slight smile as she slid her thigh on the armrest closest to Paul. "It's a bit tense in here. Enter at your own risk."

Heather shook her head as she closed the door behind them. "This is the calm stage."

Tracie's eyes widened. "You're kidding."

Ted waved them all off. "It will be over tomorrow."

"What happens tomorrow?" They were the first words Jennifer had spoken in the apartment that day.

She'd rushed out hours earlier to go shopping with Tracie and Heather. Now she slipped through the blockade formed by her female companions and stared Paul down.

He glanced at her, his gaze never touching her face. "I'm moving to a place in Mississauga."

It was clear she didn't like being ignored when she stepped right in front of him. She didn't stop until her shoes tapped against his socks. "Since when?"

This time he didn't evade her stare. "Since you kicked me out."

Tracie broke the tension by resting her hand on Paul's shoulder. "A suburb. You'll be nearby."

He didn't feel her touch. Didn't feel anything. "Yeah."

"We will still see you, right?" Tracie asked.

Ted stretched his arms along the back of the couch. "Of course. He's leaving the apartment, not the country."

Heather cleared her throat. With a head nod, she gestured to the other side of the apartment. "Tracie, help me in the kitchen."

"Okay." Tracie managed to make the word last for four syllables.

Not that Paul saw Tracie. No, he kept his focus on Jennifer.

"Ted?" Heather snapped out her boyfriend's name.

"What?" he snapped right back.

This time she pointed in the direction she wanted him to go. "You, too."

Ted glanced at the television, then at Heather. "It's the second period of the hockey game."

"Now."

Jennifer waited until Ted grumbled his way past her and left them alone. She hit the off switch on the television and plunged the room into an unnerving quiet. "You didn't tell me tomorrow was moving day."

"I figured you'd notice when you didn't see me sleeping on the couch."

"I only need some—"

"Don't." He couldn't listen to this again. He'd heard it so many times, in so many ways, and it meant only one thing—she was leaving him. Maybe not physically, and maybe not right now, but she could throw up an emotional wall faster than any woman he'd ever met.

Maybe he had jumped too fast. He'd wanted to be with her again so badly after all those calls, and after looking at those photos and reliving the memories, that he rushed to make it happen. To him, that was a good thing. It showed his commitment. But it scared the hell out of her, and he didn't know how to put that right again.

"You still don't understand," she said in a sad voice.

"You want time and space. I get it." He stood up and tried to brush past her, but she held onto his forearm.

"You're punishing me."

He looked down into those eyes that haunted his dreams. "I'm giving the lady what she wants."

Seven

PAUL HAD BEEN GONE FOR A WEEK AND SHE MISSED
him like crazy.

Jennifer knew setting a boundary was the right thing to do. He
was still an unknown quantity in so many ways, as was her future.
She was smart to be cautious.

The sentiment was right. It was her delivery that needed a huge
amount of work.

Kicking him out right after they found each other again had
sent the wrong message. Banning him from her bed had been a
huge blow to his ego. She knew because Ted told her and because
Paul's face didn't leave any room for doubt.

I didn't have anywhere to go . . .

His words about their childhood echoed back to her. She had
been trying to protect herself and she hurt him. Again.

The two calls she made to check on him since he rented the first
floor apartment had been terse on his end. She stuck to the pleas-
antries, and he barely spoke. Not exactly the best way to restart
their dating lives.

She stood now in the driveway of the townhouse on Glen Buren Drive and stared at the red front door.

Tracie sat down on the car's hood and joined in the staring. "You okay?"

"No." Jennifer wondered if she would ever feel normal again. The boy who square danced into her life seemed to have stolen her stability along with her heart.

"You did what you thought was right."

"You didn't see his face when I told him to leave."

Tracie had been there for the final blow. Paul announced his moving date and then left the apartment. He hadn't come back except to grab his bag and head out. Tracie didn't express her disappointment, but her head shaking for the rest of that day spoke pretty clearly.

"You're here now," Tracie assured Jennifer. "That will mean something."

Jennifer wasn't convinced. "I hope that's enough."

"Here's Neil."

Jennifer watched Paul's closest friend in the world drive up. He sat there, behind the wheel, letting the car idle as he stared at Paul's front door. It took another few minutes for Neil to turn off the engine and step out.

Jennifer rushed through the greetings before he could say anything to further erode her confidence. "Thanks for coming."

He nodded. "I hope I don't regret this."

She decided to take the risk and lay it out there. "I don't want to lose Paul."

Neil glanced at his feet as he kicked some loose gravel around with his sneakers. "Honestly, he doesn't see it that way."

"I know."

Tracie ran her hand up and down Jennifer's arm. "He will."

Neil shook his head as he handed over Paul's extra key. "I'll trust your female instincts on this one."

Jennifer couldn't help but laugh at that. "But those are what got me into this position."

Neil's frown never wavered. "He's trying to find his way. He just needs some time to get there."

"We both do."

Tracie tugged on Neil's arm and pulled him toward the parked cars. "And we'll let you get to it."

For the first time since he arrived, Neil smiled. "Guess we can't watch, huh?"

"I'm not really into that," Jennifer said.

"Now that's a shame."

She hitched her thumb toward the highway that ran just behind the townhouse complex. "Get out of here."

Tracie waved. "Good luck."

Yeah, Jennifer worried she was going to need a lot of it.

Paul decided he had finally lost his mind. He walked into his place after eight that evening and flicked on the family room light. He could see into the kitchen beyond and the cereal bowl he left on the counter before he headed out to the construction site that morning.

And, damn, he could smell her. It wasn't possible. Jennifer had never been here. Would never be there.

Paul rubbed his temples and cursed his decision to stay up late watching the shark special. Not that he remembered any of it. He mostly stared into space and left the television on for background noise.

Rather than think about the stretch of lonely weeks ahead, he headed for the kitchen. On the way he threw his coat on the couch Tracie had found at a flea market and bought for him for twenty dollars.

He opened the refrigerator to grab something for a sandwich when he saw his bedroom door off to his right. It was closed. He didn't shut it. No real need when a guy lived alone.

There were only a few options here. He debated calling the police until he realized he didn't have anything worth stealing. It was probably the landlady who lived upstairs, or maybe the wind caught it and he didn't notice.

Still, a guy couldn't be too careful. He abandoned the turkey that had his mouth watering and pushed the bedroom door open nice and slow. It squeaked on its hinges as it went.

He saw her bare legs first. Sprawled across his mattress, covered only by a thin sheet, Jennifer lay there with her hazel eyes watching him.

"Hi." Her greeting was so soft, he almost missed it.

He blinked a few times. When she didn't disappear in a puff of smoke, he felt safe in thinking he hadn't gone careening over the thin edge of sanity.

Still, he wanted to be sure. "Jennifer?"

"Were you expecting someone else?"

"No."

"I'd worried you'd be busy tonight."

He couldn't think about anything but the smell of her hair and the soft touch of her hands, and she thought he was dating. Sometimes he wondered if she knew him at all. "With another woman? Yeah, that's not likely to happen any time soon."

"Good."

He went for the most neutral conversation he could find. It was either that or jump on top of her and forget the pain of the last few weeks, and he wasn't ready to do that. "How did you get in?"

"The door."

He bit the inside of his mouth to keep from laughing at that. "The locked one?"

"Is this what you really want to talk about right now?"

"Only in that I need to know who to thank tomorrow for letting you break in tonight."

She lifted the sheet, revealing every curve and inch of pink skin. "I might have something better in mind."

He'd stopped breathing. Not even a whiff of air moved through him.

His sole focus centered on her, wanting her, trying not to go to her. If she hadn't shifted her legs, he might have stood there forever trapped in her spell.

"I . . . uh." He swallowed as his brain searched for the right words. For any words, actually.

"Did you want to say something?"

"What are you—"

"Isn't it obvious?"

Man, he hoped so. "I don't want any miscommunication this time."

"Come closer and we can talk it over."

"Talk?"

"Eventually."

No need to play hard to get. The woman had eyes. She knew the effect her bare body and sweet voice had on him. If she didn't, all she needed to do was glance at his pants and pick up the hint.

He grabbed the edge of his shirt and unfastened fast and hard enough to rip two buttons off. "How's this?"

"You're doing fine."

He put his knee on the bed and his hand on her flat stomach. "I aim to please."

"You usually do."

"Let's see what you think in an hour."

Two hours later, they sat at his breakfast bar. His navy robe was big enough to wrap around her twice, but she didn't even bother to belt it. She just sat and nibbled on a turkey sandwich while he poured them both a drink.

"Any chance I could get that welcome home on a regular basis?" he asked.

"Maybe."

"I was hoping for something more definitive."

"You're not listening."

He had no idea what she was talking about but didn't want to tick her off by asking. "Uh, okay."

"I told you I was kicking you out of the house, not my life or my bed."

He didn't want to fight. Not again. Not after the way she rode him until his muscles begged for mercy. "You're not the easiest woman to read."

"Here's a hint." She picked at the lunch meat. "When I say I'm going to do something, I do it."

"Like not talking to me."

She shrugged. "If it makes you feel any better, Tracie said it was juvenile."

"Yeah, well, you made your point with the silent treatment."

Jennifer dropped the food and pushed the plate away from her. "I couldn't afford to surrender. The point was too important to let it go without a fight."

"And you do like to fight."

"That's not fair."

"Maybe." When he crawled into that bed with her he'd made a silent promise not to replay this argument. He wanted to move forward, and if she was willing, they would.

But her words held in his mind until he couldn't hear anything else. "Is that how you see our relationship? You surrendering to me and my needs?"

"I'm trying to figure out what our relationship is." She peeked up at him through her silky hair. "How do you see it?"

All plans to play it cool died a hard death. "All I know is that I can't stop thinking about you. Can't seem to let you go."

"Okay."

Not exactly the warm reception he was hoping for. "Okay? That's all you've got to say?"

"It's the right answer for now."

"And tomorrow?"

She shrugged. "We'll handle each day as it comes."

"Jennifer—"

She dropped the robe off her shoulders. He saw the creamy skin and the tops of her breasts . . . and he was lost. "Right. Tomorrow."

"Now, let's concentrate on today."

"I think we found something we can agree on."

Eight

There are times when you need to follow
your head and not your heart.

—Grandma Gladys, The Duchess

"WHAT IS THAT?" PAUL PEEKED OVER HER SHOULDER at the pot on the stove.

Jennifer gave the food a final stir. "Dinner."

He slid next to her with his back against the counter. Facing her, he screwed up his mouth, letting her know what he thought of her choice. "No thanks."

"Why?"

"Looks like fish eyes."

"Oh, come on." When he raised his eyebrows but didn't say anything, she stared at the grains. "It's quinoa."

"Sounds as bad as it looks."

"It's healthy."

He reached over and slipped a beer out of the refrigerator.

"You're not selling it."

"You need to try new things."

"I'm good with what I know."

Even though they were joking—well, she was—the words echoed in her brain. Something about him being satisfied and her wanting more sounded like a blueprint for their relationship. She

64

worked as a way to pay the bills, knowing there was more out there. Something bigger. He'd been paying the bills for so long he didn't want or expect more from that part of his life.

Some days she secretly blamed him for not joining her in a thirst to know what else they could be and do. Other days she envied his calm reassurance. He worked honest and hard. That was worth something, and she hated her mental wanderings that suggested otherwise.

"Does this mean you agree?" he asked.

When he just stared at her with his handsome face wide with hope, she knew she'd missed part of the conversation. "About?"

"What I just said."

"Fill me in."

The corner of his mouth kicked up. "Admit you weren't listening to me."

She grabbed the pot off the stove and moved it to the counter to have something to do. "Of course not."

Before she could turn around or leave the room, he snuck up behind her and reached around until his hands rested on her stomach. His body rested against hers and his chin balanced on her shoulder. "It's okay to zone out now and then."

"This conversation is ridiculous," she said as she tilted her head to the side to give her better access to her neck.

His mouth found her shoulder. Her earlobe. "I think you're afraid to admit it since you frequently yell at me for not listening."

She set the pot down and turned around in his arms until she faced him. With her arms wrapped around his neck, she pulled him in closer. "I do not yell."

"Guess I'm thinking of my other girlfriend."

She leaned back and punched him in the shoulder. "Aren't you funny?"

After a beat of silence, his eyebrows straightened. "You okay?"

"Offended by your taste in food, but yes."

"You've spent a lot of time the last few days with your body here but your mind somewhere else. I just want to make sure you're . . . I don't know, content."

For him, that was a good word. It meant happy. To her, it still meant settling or at least standing still.

She kissed his chin. "I'm definitely content."

"Any chance you're also willing to make something else for dinner?"

She playfully shoved him away and turned back to the pot. "You're eating the quinoa. It will be good for you to try something new."

"That theory has never worked for me."

She feared it never would.

Months later, the sex remained smoking hot, but the same old arguments surfaced. The restless energy bubbled inside her. As much as he slid into a sense of contentment, Jennifer longed to try new things.

She loved going to the office and working with her coworkers on targeted sales plans for new household products. She craved her time alone with Paul. But the wide-open world kept nibbling at her heels. There was something else out there. The knowledge radiated through her and blocked out everything else.

"Do you think we fight more than most couples?" Jennifer asked as she watched Paul read the sports page in the morning newspaper.

He didn't even look up. "You do."

"Meaning?"

"I'm just sitting here."

"Refusing to engage is fighting."

He snuck a peek at her over the top of the paper. "Actually, it's not."

"That's not true."

"So now we're fighting about what counts as fighting?" Amusement laced through his voice. "Did you run out of logical things to pick at?"

He made her argument sound ridiculous when he said it like that. She stuck to it anyway. "No."

"Problem is, you won't just let yourself be satisfied and happy as is."

She dropped her hand through the paper, crumpling it into a ball against the counter and uncovering his sleepy face to her stare. "What do you want from life?"

"You."

The fact he answered so fast and so sure brought the guilt racing up to meet her. She looked out on the horizon of her future and saw opportunities and possibilities. She often thought about his life view as limited. He didn't ask for much or want much. On her most uncharitable days, she saw it as a lack of ambition. Today she envied his grounding.

"I mean, for yourself."

"Same answer." The fact he sat there and answered in a clear voice confirmed he didn't have a need to reach outside his insular world.

"You're happy to go from job to job, play the drums in clubs now and then, and hang out with friends." Her assessment carried a slap, but she couldn't pull the words once they were out there.

"I take it you disapprove."

"I didn't say that." She knew she didn't have to. The unspoken words hung between them, building an even bigger wall to their happiness.

"Is my life and what I want really so bad?"

She glanced out the kitchen window and saw the snow fall into steep piles outside his townhouse. In a few hours he would throw on a down coat and wool hat and head outside to shovel. He'd revel in the labor, in working with his hands in the brisk air and seeing what he'd accomplished. He was decent and hardworking . . . and not what she needed right now.

The realization made her stomach flop. "What if there's more out there and you're missing it?" she asked.

"Like?"

"I don't know."

"That's not a particularly compelling argument."

She watched the neighbor struggle to free his rear tires from the ice packed around them as she fought to find the right words to express her thoughts. "I know."

Paul reached out and slipped his fingers through hers. His thumb caressed the back of her hand. "Explain to me why we can't find whatever it is you're seeking together. Why do you insist this *something* is out there and you have to be alone to find it?"

A reasonable answer escaped her. "I don't want to just get by."

"You want to experience and learn." He dropped her hand and sat back. "Yeah, I've heard this all before."

"I'm talking about me."

"Us.

"This isn't about you."

"It's about how you think I'm not adult enough for you. That I'm not ready for these grand plans you have in your head."

She looked at him then. Saw sadness in eyes that usually danced when she walked into the room and wondered why her brain insisted on throwing it all away. "Are you ready to grow up?"

"This is all because I bought a lottery ticket when I picked up the paper?"

"Of course not." It went so much deeper, and she couldn't figure out a way to make him understand that.

It was a symbol of how they led their lives. When he stumbled across a few extra dollars, he played a hunch. She got money and tried to think of a way to stretch it into this magical adventure that would stay in her heart forever.

He blew out a long agitated breath. "I'm tired."

"Right." What had she expected? They'd spent most of the evening making love and were not in the right state of mind to deal with the tough decisions they had to make. "We can talk about this later."

He wove his fingers together and clenched them until his knuckles turned white. "I mean of this conversation. It exhausts me every time we have it. You want something—something you can't even define—and when I can't figure out how to get it for you, you pick a fight."

"That's not true."

His palms fell open. "Then just tell me what you need from me."

Everything . . . nothing. She really didn't know the solution for finding the right guy at fifteen, before she was prepared for him or had lived the life she wanted to live.

"This really isn't about you," she whispered, hoping he'd believe her this time.

He raised his hand. "Hold up."

"It's about—"

"Stop."

The words died on her lips. "Okay."

"You want to go off and find yourself, or whatever you call it. Fine. Do it. But don't hide behind some dumbass line guys fall back on to dump women who cling too hard."

"That's not what I was doing."

"If you need to leave, then go."

A hot ball of grief lodged in her throat. "I don't want to."

"Honestly, Jennifer. You don't know what the hell you want." He cocked his head to the side and stared at her as if he was reasoning out the world's problem. "Strike that. You know one thing. You know I'm not enough for you."

Right now. The words echoed through her as her heart shredded in half. She could hear the ripping in her ears and feel the tear right through her skin. She looked down at her pink slippers, half expecting to see blood on the floor.

"All I'm asking for is some time," she said.

He slid off the stool and stood up. "You can have it. Take all you need."

Every cell inside her screamed to grab onto him and not let go. "I don't want to lose you."

He stopped as he hit the doorway to his bedroom. "I'm not going to hold you where you don't want to be."

"It's not like that."

"It is." He rubbed his eyes, stared at the ceiling—did everything he could not to glance in her direction. "Remember one thing."

"What?"

"I'm not the one who walked away. One day I might not be here when you come back." Then he slipped into the bedroom and closed the door behind him.

Nine

If you need to move on, move on.
Don't dawdle.

—Grandma Gladys, The Duchess

JENNIFER CRIED FOR THREE DAYS. THIS MORNING SHE moved like a zombie and wished she lacked a heart like one.

Heather shoved a bowl of granola in front of her sister. "Jennifer, you have to eat something."

Tracie hovered in the doorway with her keys in her hand. "I can go out and get—"

"I'm not hungry." Jennifer appreciated the concern and the coddling, but she needed to grieve. And the idea of eating made her queasy. Doing anything sounded pretty awful.

"This isn't healthy." Heather played with the spoon, letting it clank against the side of the bowl.

"And you're the dumper, not the dumpee."

Heather shot their friend a wide-eyed, what-the-hell look. "Tracie, that's not helping."

"It's the truth." Tracie took the seat across from Jennifer. "Isn't this what you want? You asked for space, and he gave it to you. I don't see the problem."

"Yes . . ." Jennifer shook her head. "No."

Leaving Paul had never been the point. Hurting him burned a hole through her stomach. The tightness across his cheeks and pained expression on his lips. She had a hard time handling all of it.

The second he'd stepped into the bedroom after their argument and shut her out, all she wanted to do was run to him and apologize. Only the fear of sending him a horrible mixed message and cutting him even deeper had kept her rooted to the same spot in his kitchen for hours.

She'd waited until the snow piled up and the wind howled. When he finally slipped into the bathroom without looking at her, she'd snuck out with only her clothes and her purse.

He'd had Neil deliver the stuff she'd left at his house. Seeing the bag sitting just inside her front door had touched off a second round of regret and dragging despair.

"If you can't love him back you need to let him move on."

Tracie repeated the same theory Jennifer said over and over in her own head. It proved just as frustrating when it came from someone else.

"I have to agree on this one." Heather took Jennifer's hand and squeezed until she got eye contact. "Look, I adore Paul. Hell, I've pushed you together since you were fifteen. But there's clearly a disconnect between you. Something you're not getting. It might be kinder to let him go."

Jennifer wanted to work up a good case of fury against her sister and fight off her words, then lash out at the world. Instead, she told the truth. "When I'm with him, it's perfect."

"It is not," Tracie shot back.

This was the part Jennifer couldn't explain even to herself. Paul was right that she pushed him and kept at it until their words blew into a full-fledged fight. But in those quiet moments when they were making dinner or snuggling on the couch, there was nowhere else she wanted to be.

Her dreams dropped away. And that's what scared the hell out of her.

They were too immature and untested to head into a lifetime that came with settling down too early. They needed to grow, and she prayed they'd someday weave their lives back together. More importantly, she hoped he would see her points and ultimately forgive her for pushing him aside.

"It's when I try something new, like when we went to that oxygen bar, or when I go out for drinks with people from work, or meet an executive from an advertising firm and he asks me out." She searched for the right way to say it. "It's like for that split second I'm tempted to be someone else."

Tracie's eyes narrowed in the disapproving scowl she'd perfected as the older sister of four brothers. "So all of this is because you want to date other people?"

Jennifer shook her head. That's the part that never fit together in her mind. "No."

"Are you sure?" Tracie asked.

"I would never cheat on Paul."

"Then what?" Tracie spun the full cereal bowl around on the table.

Jennifer barely heard the thumping as the edges hit the wood. "I can't figure out why it's always so hard for us."

"Maybe it's not supposed to be easy." Heather reached out and grabbed the bowl, putting it out of handling distance. "Maybe a relationship worth keeping takes more than that."

"Probably." Jennifer just said the word to fill in the gap.

"Isn't that what the Duchess always told us? You put the time in and get out so much more."

Tracie pressed her lips together. "Or maybe you're just not ready."

Jennifer picked the option that didn't carry a weight of guilt and judgment. If the answer depended on measure of effort, that would mean she really did bail, just as Paul accused her of doing. "I think that's it."

Tracie glanced at Heather before she spoke. "Then let him go and move on. You both deserve that."

They did. She did. He certainly did. But knowing and acting were two different things for Jennifer. "I don't know if I can."

Neil sat down at the opposite end of the couch and handed a beer to Paul. The game blared on the television and snacks littered the coffee table in front of them.

It was the first time Paul had ventured out of the house to do more than work or shovel out the driveway as his rental agreement required. Neil's house was safe. It was a Jennifer-free space. No photos of her. No memories of her there, since she'd never been inside.

Beer, a remote control and unhealthy food. The place was a guy's haven. Now if Paul could only get his best friend to stop looking at him like a worried grandmother.

"What?" Paul asked without taking his eyes off the screen.

"You okay?"

"Do I look okay?"

"Kind of like dogshit, actually."

Paul smiled at that one. He knew it was true. He barely recognized the unshaven guy who greeted him in the mirror that morning. "Thanks."

"Look, this isn't a big deal." Neil shifted in his seat and balanced his arm on the back of the couch.

"Did you miss the part where she left me because I'm . . . forget it. I really don't know what the issue was." Paul had lost count of the number of times he turned their conversations over his head, trying to find the answer. Trying to figure out a way to keep her from walking out on him in search of something better.

"It's what you guys do."

Paul stared at his friend. "What the hell does that mean?"

Neil held up his hands as if ready to block any blows that came his way. "Only that you guys have broken up before. This is not new."

Paul balanced the bottle on his lap and leaned his head against the cushion behind him. "Not by my choice."

"Yeah, well, women tend to drive these things. The good news is she keeps circling back around to you."

"Not this time."

"Come on. That's the beer talking."

"She's moving on."

The thought of her with another guy, of someone else spending time with her, watching movies with her on the couch. Another man touching her body and kissing those lips. The visual images drove him to madness.

Letting her walk out meant conceding she would go to another guy eventually. His brain fought the possibility as his stomach heaved.

"You don't know that you're over." Neil peeled the label on his bottle. "Besides, Jennifer strikes me as faithful."

"When we're together, sure."

"See?"

"We're not now."

"You've thought that before."

"It feels different." The break-up sat on his chest, pressing him down until he nearly choked from the force of it.

"How?"

Maybe they never said the actual words, but her eyes had said good-bye. "Not sure."

"Then—"

"I can't figure out how to hold onto her with a grip that doesn't scare the crap out of her."

Or how to let her go.

There it was. They couldn't come up with a way to stay together, but their connection of years and memories refused to let them break apart in a clean and tolerable way.

"You met young," Neil said.

"That seems like it should be a good thing." Paul spent a lot of time wondering if he'd known then the never-ending sensual dance they would engage in throughout the years, how Jennifer would take his heart and never stop squeezing, if he would have walked away when Heather tried to introduce them. It was a matter of self-preservation.

Neil scoffed. "Nothing good comes out of high school. You of all people should know that."

"School sucked, and I sucked at it."

"Yeah, you had other things on your mind. Like figuring out where to sleep and how you were going to eat."

Paul refused to dwell on those dark days. Being adopted and handed a bad hand was no excuse. Other people had it worse and got by. He survived and vowed never to hide behind the tough times or let them color everything else. Despite everything, he'd kept that promise.

Except where Jennifer was concerned. He couldn't puzzle through her no matter how hard he tried. "But I'm a grown man now. I should be able to figure this out."

"Do you forget there's a woman involved? Bless their sexy little bodies, but they are pure trouble."

"No kidding."

"They twist you up . . . man, they hold all the power, and that bugs the shit out of me."

"I can't take it anymore."

"I know, dude." Neil shook his head in a moment of male-to-male sympathy.

Paul reached in his back pocket and pulled out his wallet. He handed a folded piece of colored paper to Neil. "Check this out."

"What is it?"

"Scratch off lottery ticket."

Neil smoothed it out and stared at it. Then his eyes widened. "Sweet damn, you won."

"Ironic, isn't it?"

Neil's smile froze. "What do you mean?"

"She dumps me and I get ten thousand dollars."

"Maybe your luck is turning."

"Doubt it."

Neil threw the ticket on the table. "Then maybe it's the universe's way of giving you a consolation prize."

Paul had already come to that conclusion. "I'd rather have the girl."

Ten

*Try new things, grab every opportunity
but stay true to who you are.*

—Grandma Gladys, The Duchess

THEY HADN'T OFFICIALLY DATED FOR MONTHS. JENNIFER symbolically cut the ties with Paul by moving out of her apartment and into a cozy cottage on a tree-lined street in Toronto. The small space was soothing and warm.

Heather and Tracie joined in the start-over relocation. They'd packed up everything they owned, painted the walls in calming blue tones, and filled the rooms with a mix of flea market finds and family hand-me-downs.

Tonight the usually quiet house was packed. Music thumped in the background, and cool air moved through the open front and back door.

Tracie loved to celebrate her birthday big and this year was no exception. Men gathered on the back patio around the beer and argued about a play in some game that Jennifer didn't care about. A few couples wandered in and out of the kitchen carrying small plates and whispering with their heads close together as couples tend to do.

Tracie grabbed Jennifer's arm before she could try a piece of cake. They moved into the small hallway that led to the bedrooms. Tracie's sense of urgency had Jennifer worrying something awful had happened.

"What's wrong?" Jennifer asked.

"I'm sorry."

"For what?"

"Paul."

Just hearing his name sent a shot of longing spinning through her. He claimed that she was cold and distant, that she cut him off and didn't care about his feelings. Maybe she deserved the emotional beating, but she never felt the detachment he accused her of.

She'd spent hours pouring over photos and remembering the good times. More than once she had to put down the phone and walk out of the room to keep from calling him.

But Tracie knew how much Jennifer missed him and wouldn't mention his name with good reason. "What are you talking about?"

"I think she's apologizing for me showing up before she could warn you." Paul's deep voice broke into the intimate girl chat.

Jennifer's head shot up. She took in his jeans and black blazer, the hair ruffled by the breeze and shoulders broad enough to block out the room behind him. The color in his face made him look sun-kissed despite the chilly early spring days. Whatever he did with his time now, he did most of it outside. It suited him because he looked calmer than she'd seen him in a long time.

She searched her mind for the right greeting, the perfect blend of welcome and cool. When that failed, she went with the standard. "Hi."

The sexy smile she knew so well crossed his lips. For a second, all of the fights faded into the background and she remembered the sweet boy who charmed everyone.

He slipped his hands into the back pockets of his pants. "Guess I'm a surprise."

"I know this isn't ideal, but he's a friend and—" Tracie stepped between them with her hand on Paul's chest.

For some reason, the protective move ticked Jennifer off. Her dear friend was watching out for him. As if an explosion were imminent and he needed a guardian. Him and not her.

"This is ridiculous. We're not enemies." Jennifer did a little subtle pushing of her own and slid to Paul's side.

His smile widened. "Never that."

At his calm reassurance, the muscles across her shoulders relaxed. She leaned over and kissed him on the check, ignoring the guy who pushed past them on the way to the bathroom.

As soon as Paul's familiar, comforting scent hit her senses, she pulled back. "I'm happy to see you."

His gaze made a quick tour of her body, heating every inch in its wake. "You look good."

"You don't look too bad yourself."

"Always nice to hear that from a woman."

Tracie's gaze moved between Paul and Jennifer in fast beats. "I guess I should go check on everyone."

Paul nodded. "We'll be fine. No bloodshed on the new floors. I promise."

That they even had to deal with Tracie's intrusion confused Jennifer. She got the distinct impression her friend had come to a disturbing conclusion: Paul was the wronged party. There was no other reason for the scowling and hovering.

When the silence drew out too long, Jennifer filled the void. "You still doing construction?"

"I'm about to start some hydro utility work. I've got a four-month stint, so I'll be in and out until the contract is done. The hope is that it turns into full time."

A focus. He'd found a solid job with solid pay. She was happy for him even as a kick of regret landed in her stomach. "Sounds hard but fulfilling."

"It's dependable, and that's all that mattered to me when I took it." He leaned his shoulder against the doorjamb and pressed in closer to her. "You?"

"I'm doing event coordination now."

"Okay, I can pretend otherwise, but I really have no idea what that is."

They both laughed, and just like that the odd tension crackling around them evaporated. This was Paul. He knew every inch of her and had either lived through or heard every embarrassing story. Through everything, she'd always believed he wanted her to succeed and this time was no exception.

"I set up meetings and conferences. Run them. There's some travel, but that's not a bad thing."

"You'd be good at that."

"Why do you think so?"

He shrugged. "You're friendly. People like you."

"I tend to be someone who hovers in the background." Shy was the word she'd always used to describe herself.

"You shine as soon as you're comfortable."

His words filled her with a giddiness that reminded her of seeing him for the first time at fifteen. "Still the sweet talker."

"Still beautiful."

If his voice hadn't slipped into a husky growl against her senses she never would have asked the question. But it did, so she gave in. "Do you still like me?"

"Can you really not tell?"

She didn't realize how much she missed him until she stood by his side locked in silly conversation. The comfort of just being together was a gift she missed. "I'm happy you came tonight."

"I almost didn't, but Tracie insisted it would be okay."

"Tracie."

He leaned in as if he were sharing top secret information. "Your best friend."

"Yeah, I know who she is."

The need to change the topic swamped Jennifer. "Want some cake?"

He barked out a laugh that bent him double. "That is not what I thought you were going to say next."

This is the Paul she loved—bawdy and totally at ease with his sexuality. He didn't play games or pretend. When he wanted something, he said it.

"Where is your mind?" she asked once he stopped laughing.

"You don't want to know."

But part of her did and always would. "Maybe I should get you some ice water instead."

He lifted an arm toward the kitchen. "Lead on."

It took hours for the house to quiet down and the crowds to clear. Paul lay on the couch, wearing nothing more than his underwear and a tee, and stared at the dark ceiling.

He should have stayed a few minutes at the party and then cleared out. Hung around for just enough time to keep Tracie from being upset. That had been his great plan.

Jennifer's sexy black dress caused the problem. She showed off those long legs that sent him over the edge every time she wrapped them around him. One look at her silky hair and take-me-to-the-bedroom smile and he was a goner.

Not that staying and crashing on the couch made an ounce of sense. The self-imposed torture of laying right down the hall from her made him wonder if he had grown up at all since he'd last seen her. He was alone in the family room with a blanket and a flat pillow. Not exactly his idea of a hot night.

He closed his eyes, but a rustling noise had him opening them again. He could make out Jennifer's silhouette in the shadows. She stood at the end of the couch with her hands folded in front of her.

It was as if thinking about her had made her materialize. But this was better than a dream. This was flesh and blood real. And when she walked toward him, his lower half jumped to life.

He slipped his arm behind his head so he could lift up and get a better look at her. He thought about throwing her a line but stayed quiet. She was stalking, seducing, and he was not about to mess that up by saying something stupid.

She stopped next to him, next to the hand at his side. From this short distance, he could see her bare legs, all pale and lean, peeking out from under a nightgown that barely covered her most interesting parts. Before he could reach out and touch it, she shifted and the material swept to the floor.

Not even his fantasies worked out this well.

His gaze moved over her naked body. Slim hips and high breasts. She was so damn sexy it hurt not to touch her. Then she was lifting the blanket and sliding over him.

Her fingers dipped into the waistband of his underwear as her lips pressed against his collarbone. In the silence she caressed and enticed him. Her hot mouth, her soft hands. She had his neck lengthening and his head pressing into the pillow. When he caught his breath again, he lifted his mouth and found hers.

The kiss set off fireworks in his skull. Every nerve in his body snapped to life. He was aware of her smell and her scent, her legs as they straddled him and her fingers as they peeled down his underwear.

They didn't speak. Didn't need to. This rhythm was as natural to them as breathing. They'd made love so many times that words were no longer necessary.

It was the talking and thinking that killed him . . . so he didn't try either.

A half hour later, she sat up and grabbed her nightgown off the floor and slipped it over her head. "No matter how hard I try or how determined I am, I can't stay away from you."

He trailed his hand down her back as his muscles recharged. "We're even, because I can't say no to you."

"What does that say about us, do you think?" She peeked over her shoulder and stared down at him with soft hazel eyes filled with confusion. "Really, I want to know because I don't understand it."

That made two of them. When it came to explaining this, he was as lost as she was. "No idea."

"Hmmm."

His body had barely cooled when his brain whirred to life. The truth hit him as hard as his attraction for her. "I just know we can't keep doing this."

"I know." She stood up. Took five steps, then turned around.

"It's killing me not to be with you. To get this close and then watch you walk away."

"I never meant to hurt you."

"And I know that, too. On some level. On the days when I'm not furious or frustrated." His eyes had adjusted to the darkness and he saw her clearly. Pain hovered on the mouth he had spent so much time kissing and loving.

She didn't say anything for more than a minute. Neither did he.

As the house creaked from the wind blowing outside, she cleared her throat. "You should date other people."

"I have been."

Her head snapped back. "Oh."

If he were standing, he would have kicked his own ass. The slap of the words sounded harder than he meant. He took out other women to forget Jennifer. It was that simple.

But he couldn't admit that part without shredding what was left of his ego. "I didn't mean for it to come out that way."

She shook her head, even held up a hand as if she could block his words. "It's okay. I deserve that."

He pushed up on one elbow. "It wasn't a punishment."

"Okay."

He needed her to get this much at least. "Just a statement. It's truth. I need you to know I'm not sitting here waiting for you to come back."

"Anybody special?"

"Only you."

"When you say things like that . . ."

No, absolutely not. He couldn't wander down that road only for her to throw up another block and turn him around. "You're free, Jennifer. I'm not holding you or trying to manipulate you."

"I get that."

"You snuck into my bed tonight, not vice versa."

"And other nights."

"Yeah."

She backed up until she leaned against the wall. A heavy sigh shook her body. "One day there might be someone else with you, and there won't be a place for me."

"There should be. We both deserve to find what we need because we're over." That slap he meant because it was true.

If the words hurt her, she didn't show it. Her body stayed slack, as if she'd been beaten up and waited for surrender. "Then why does it feel so unfinished?"

The description was so painful yet so true. "I'm guessing that's how it will always be for us."

"Undone."

The word fit. Hurt like hell, but fit. "You should go back to your own bed, Jennifer."

"Yeah." But she didn't move.

Since he couldn't handle her standing there, he pushed. "Good night, Jennifer."

"Good night, Paul."

Amazing how that word sounded so much like good-bye in his head.

Eleven

Nothing cuts as deep as disloyalty.

—Grandma Gladys, The Duchess

"I DON'T KNOW IF I COULD DO IT," ADAM SAID AS JENNIFER slid into the car seat next to him.

They'd spent the evening laughing over Greek food. It was a pattern they'd repeated often since they started casually hanging out together. They weren't more than friends and never would be, but it was nice to go to dinner and not worry about the usual date stuff. With Adam, Jennifer could be herself and not worry about anything other than talking.

He was tall and dark and made her laugh, but he never shifted from the friend category to anything more. She'd given her heart once, and there was nothing left to share in that department.

"Paul and I are long over." She pulled the seatbelt across her stomach with a bit more force than she intended. The subject of Paul tended to do that to her.

"I don't mean you, babe. I mean him." Adam started the car. The steady thump of the windshield wiper filled the space. "You guys used to date, and now he walks into your house and sees me there, waiting for you. Even though there's nothing to be jealous about, he doesn't know that."

"And?"

"Just saying that can't be easy on a guy."

"Paul is fine." She reached over and turned up the radio.

Adam turned it back down. "You'd be a hard woman to lose."

"Thank you."

Adam knew pieces of the story but not all of it. Jennifer owed Paul that small bit of confidentiality. She had only shared the deepest moments and fears with Heather and Tracie. Only they knew that Paul was the love of her life.

"I'm just saying I feel bad for the guy." Adam rubbed his hands together and blew on them twice before returning them to the steering wheel.

"You were using the phone, not walking around the kitchen naked." A chill moved through her as she watched the raindrops splash in a puddle.

"You know what I mean."

She did. She'd grown accustomed to coming home and seeing Paul there. He'd been friends with Tracie for years and had a strong relationship with Heather. It wasn't fair to ask him to walk away from those contacts when they split up.

Almost six months had passed since the birthday party. They'd kept everything friendly and hands-off since then. Despite that, having Paul stand there when Adam escorted her out the door earlier made a nerve at the base of her back thump.

"We're over. Paul agrees." She made that comment in her head every week. Maybe saying it out loud to Adam would give it some strength.

"You don't have to convince me."

No, but if she said it enough she might believe it. "Then why are we arguing about it?"

Adam flashed her a grin. "I thought we were just talking."

They pulled out of the parking lot and headed for her house a few blocks away. They normally would have walked the short distance, but the rain made a stroll impossible.

She rubbed her forehead as the minutes passed. "Sorry. Don't mean to be defensive tonight."

"Maybe you need to go to bed."

"I do."

Adam turned the car into her driveway and shut off the engine. He shifted in his seat and stared at her. "You don't have to try so hard, you know."

"I enjoy being with you."

"Same here, but that's not what I mean."

She leaned back against the headrest. "I know. I just don't understand why the Paul thing doesn't get easier. Ending it was my decision."

Adam glanced at the street and nodded in the direction of Paul's car. "He's still here."

"He and Tracie planned to watch a movie."

"They do that sort of thing a lot?"

"Paul comes in and out all the time." Seeing him so often should have made Jennifer uncomfortable. Instead, it filled her with an odd sense of security.

"You okay with all that contact?"

"For now."

Paul thought he should sit up. At the very least, he should take another chair and let Tracie have the couch. He sure as hell shouldn't be sitting there with her arm wrapped around his shoulders and her body pressed up against his.

Not that her move had been a total surprise. Tracie had been dropping hints for weeks that she wanted more from him. Neil insisted Tracie had started plotting long before that. Maybe, but Paul was too bound to Jennifer back then to notice.

But they were over now. He had dated women since it ended with Jennifer. No one special and nothing long-term. Just fun and a few dinners. He and Jennifer had talked about this. They could save their friendship and hang out without more. No matter how tempting she was.

Tracie dragged her hand through the hair at the back of his neck as she whispered in his ear. "Maybe we should finish this in my room."

He was free. This wasn't cheating. He repeated the refrain in his head until he couldn't hear anything else.

"Paul?"

Tracie had been a good friend, so supportive and sweet in the days following his final relationship implosion with Jennifer. He cared about Tracie. Liked her short blonde hair and found her attractive. But he didn't want to lead her on.

"I'm thinking we need to keep things the way they are," he said, knowing it was not only the right answer but the only one.

"We could have so much more."

"And mess it all up."

Her hand pressed his head toward hers. "Or it could be great."

She wanted him to kiss her.

He wanted to bolt.

Right as her lips met his cheek, the front door swung open. Tracie froze against him as his body went into shutdown mode.

READER RESPONSE CARD

We care about your opinions! Please take a moment to fill out our Reader Survey online at **http://survey.hcibooks.com**. To show our appreciation, we'll give you an **instant discount coupon** for future book purchases, as well as a special gift available only online.

If you prefer, you may mail this survey card back to us and receive a discount coupon by mail. All answers are confidential.

(PLEASE PRINT IN ALL CAPS)

First Name _____ Last Name _____

Address _____ Email _____

City _____ State _____ Zip _____

1. Gender
- ☐ Female ☐ Male

2. Age
- ☐ Under 20
- ☐ 21-30 ☐ 31-40
- ☐ 41-50 ☐ 51-60
- ☐ Over 60

3. Marital Status
- ☐ Married ☐ Single

4. How you did get this book?
- ☐ Received as gift
- ☐ Bought for myself
- ☐ Borrowed from a friend
- ☐ Borrowed from my library

5. If bought for yourself, how did you find out about it?
- ☐ Recommendation
- ☐ Store Display
- ☐ Read about it on a Website
- ☐ Email message or e-newsletter
- ☐ Book review or author interview

6. How many books do you read a year, excluding educational material?
- ☐ 4 or less ☐ 5-8
- ☐ 9-12 ☐ 12 or more

7. Do you have children under the age of 18 at home?
- ☐ Yes ☐ No

8. What type of romance do you enjoy most?
- ☐ Contemporary
- ☐ Historical
- ☐ Paranormal
- ☐ Erotic
- ☐ All types

9. What are your sensuality preferences?
- ☐ Wild and erotic
- ☐ Steamy but moderate
- ☐ Sweet and sensual
- ☐ Doesn't matter as long as it fits the story

10. Where do you usually buy books?
- ☐ Online (amazon.com, etc.)
- ☐ Bookstore chain (Borders, B&N...)
- ☐ Independent/local bookstore
- ☐ Big Box store (Target, Wal-Mart...)
- ☐ Drug Store or Supermarket

11. How often do you read romance novels?
- ☐ Every now and then
- ☐ Several times a year
- ☐ Constantly

FOLD HERE

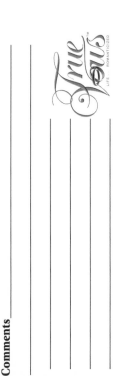

12. What influences you most when purchasing a book?
(Rank each from 1 to 5 with 1 being the top)

	1	2	3	4	5
Author	1	2	3	4	5
Price	1	2	3	4	5
Title	1	2	3	4	5
Reviews	1	2	3	4	5
Cover Design	1	2	3	4	5
Series/Publisher	1	2	3	4	5
Recommendation	1	2	3	4	5

13. Annual household income
- ☐ Under $25,000
- ☐ $25,000–$40,000
- ☐ $41,000–$50,000
- ☐ $51,000–$75,000
- ☐ Over $75,000

14. How long have you been reading romance novels?
- ☐ 1–2 years   ☐ 3–5 years
- ☐ More than 5 years

Comments

15. What other topics do you enjoy reading?

Non-Fiction
- ☐ Family/parenting
- ☐ Relationships
- ☐ Addictions/Recovery
- ☐ Health/nutrition
- ☐ Cooking
- ☐ Religious
- ☐ Spirituality
- ☐ Inspiration/affirmations
- ☐ Self-improvement
- ☐ Sports
- ☐ Pets
- ☐ Memoirs
- ☐ True Crime

Fiction
- ☐ Mystery
- ☐ Chick-lit
- ☐ Historical
- ☐ Paranormal

When the silence didn't break and the scent of rain rolled in through the open front door, he looked up. Jennifer stood, eyes wide and hand clenched on the doorknob. She hadn't moved or tried to step inside. Rain pounded over her, soaking her hair and dripping to the floor from her beige coat.

Tracie groaned and buried her forehead in his shoulder.

Paul couldn't move. Only the rush of blood to his face let him know his body still functioned. Words failed him. He couldn't think of an excuse and wasn't sure he should have to.

But that look. Jennifer's eyes mirrored blinding shock, and despair played on every inch of her face.

After a few minutes, she broke the silence by shutting the door with a soft click. The stare down continued. When her gaze focused on his face, he showed her the respect of not turning away. It wasn't until she went into her bedroom that he realized the final shot, if one had ever existed, was now gone.

This wasn't just about them. Tracie had gotten sucked into this round.

Tracie finally lifted her head. "Are you okay?"

The words broke through, bringing the answer with a rush of clarity. He hadn't done anything wrong . . . so why did he feel like crap? "Yeah."

"Sure?"

"This isn't going to happen." He disengaged from her hold and shifted away until a few inches separated them on the couch.

She turned frantic. Her hands slipped around as she talked and her words rushed together. "Don't make a decision now."

"There's only one answer."

"Jennifer dumped you." The panic cleared from Tracie's face. "Move on."

Amazing how those words buzz sawed right through him. "I may not understand much about women—"

She crossed her arms over her chest and flopped back against the sofa cushions. "Obviously."

"But I know this triangle is a catastrophe waiting to happen."

"Let me worry about that."

"It's not just about you."

"You're talking about Jennifer."

"I'm talking about me going home." He stood up. "Good night, Tracie."

"You walked in on them?" Heather asked as she paced the small space in front of Jennifer's bedroom window.

"Yes." Jennifer wrapped her arms around her knees and curled into a ball near her headboard. She tried not to touch her eyes. They burned from the inside out, all itchy and swollen. She knew without looking they resembled rare hamburger.

Heather pivoted. "On the couch. Our couch."

"Yes."

"In our house." With every phrase, Heather's voice grew louder. Her feet pounded against the floor and her hands balled into fists. Fury poured off of her.

"She was all over him."

Heather stopped. "Technically, that's not his fault."

"He wasn't fighting her off." That part stung the most. Jennifer didn't even have to close her eyes to replay the scene.

Then her imagination took over. Visions of Paul holding Tracie, touching her. Paul kissing Tracie. She didn't know if any of that had happened, but the film playing in her head held the images. Jennifer almost gagged on them.

"You should kill her." Heather nodded as she glared at the closed door to the rest of the cottage. "I'll help you."

"It's more tempting than you know." Jennifer had spent most of the night devising ways to hurt Tracie.

Jennifer had never been moved to violence . . . until now. She hated injustice. As a kid she'd failed a class rather than show respect to a teacher who allowed bullying. People had to earn her trust, and Tracie had. Now she had violated it in the most fundamental way.

There was a girl code. A friendship line you never crossed. Tracie knew the truth, knew that Jennifer had lost her heart to Paul years before. Ignoring that and moving in made Jennifer want to pound something.

Heather dropped on the edge of the bed. "What about him?"

Jennifer tried to calm her breathing, but the hate festering inside unleashed and refused to be chained again. "What do you mean?"

"Do we hate him this morning, too?"

She was disappointed and sad, certainly heartsick, but she didn't really blame him. "I wish."

"Are you sure?"

"No." But she wanted to. With her heart smashed, she wanted him to feel the same. "We'd agreed to see other people. I'd be a complete hypocrite if I questioned Paul's fidelity."

"Besides, you don't know if anything really happened. You said it looked kind of one-sided."

"Or I want to think that." If when she dated other guys Paul felt half of the misery she experienced now, she'd messed up huge. This kind of hurt, the rip-your-guts-out-and-stomp-on-them kind, rivaled the pain of their final break-up.

"The one thing we can agree on is that Tracie swooped in with some sort of mucked-up attempt to win Paul over." Heather shook her head. "That makes me furious with her and, well, with him. Can't he see through that?"

"This isn't about him. It's about a friend of more than fifteen years stabbing me." The pain in Jennifer's stomach felt as if each word had been ripped out of her. "She didn't even talk to me or tell me she was attracted to him. No, she saw an opening and went for it."

Heather nodded. "I definitely hate her on your behalf."

This tainted every moment of their friendship. Jennifer questioned every previous detail; she'd spent the long evening hours hunting for signs of Tracie's true feelings for Paul. She didn't have to go far. The hints lined up—always touching him, buying him things, whining about how it was fairer to let him go—Tracie was guilty of every offense. Jennifer wondered how she'd missed all the signs.

"Tracie knows what Paul means to me. Even if he's my past, he's the one guy who is off-limits, or should be."

"No argument here." Heather leaned over with her elbows balanced on her knees and stared at the floor. "Are you going to confront her?"

"No."

Heather's head snapped up. "Why the hell not?"

Jennifer had turned the possibility over in her mind. She wanted to scream and rage, but none of that could make her unsee what she'd seen. She couldn't grab back that moment and make it never happen.

"Not going to give her the satisfaction." She tightened her fist over the tissue she'd stuffed there and said the words that hurt the most. "The reality is, it's not my business."

"Don't let her off the hook with that. She needs to know how you feel and how crappy this is."

"Oh, I'm not going to forgive and forget. No way. The friendship is over, and we'll never get it back." Jennifer didn't want it back. She wasn't even sure she could stand in the same room with Tracie without throwing something at her.

"You're taking this entirely too well."

Jennifer lifted her head so her sister could see the eyes that hurt even to blink. "Look closer."

Heather winced. "Right."

After a short knock, the bedroom door opened. Tracie peeked around the corner. "Hi."

Her nerve touched off another round of mind-numbing fury inside Jennifer. How dare Tracie walk in as if she were welcome? The idea that she didn't know the extent of her betrayal was too hard to imagine.

"Have a good night?"

At Heather's whack of sarcasm, Tracie swallowed. "Jennifer, can we—"

No way. "No."

"Excuse me?"

Jennifer threw her legs off the bed and stood up. It was a miracle her muscles held her weight. She felt boneless and empty and shaky enough to fall right back down. "I have to get ready to go out."

No way would she let Tracie know the day's plans consisted of crying and grieving in the bedroom. Then searching the newspaper for a new place to live.

Tracie's hand tightened on the edge of the door. "We should talk. It wasn't what you think."

Jennifer just stared. She stood there and faced down the woman she once considered her best friend and didn't say a word.

She waited until Tracie started squirming and glancing around the room, like she had a vain hope there might be something there that would save her.

"Talk about what, Tracie?" Her ability to hold her voice steady filled Jennifer with pride. Shaking or breaking down were not options. "What could we possibly have to say to each other right now? I can't think of a thing."

"I just—"

Jennifer felt the fury rush through her blood. "What? Say it."

The silence dragged on until Tracie swallowed. "Nothing, I guess."

Jennifer felt her first taste of satisfaction. "That's right."

Twelve

Remember to take pleasure in the small things because they can sometimes mean everything.

—Grandma Gladys, The Duchess

BEING THE BIGGER PERSON SUCKED. JENNIFER CAME to that conclusion as she walked into the barn at their friend Ed's farm in Coldwater.

As the weeks after the incident stretched into months, Jennifer's anger only festered. Paul and Tracie hung out all the time. While Jennifer never saw or heard anything that suggested their friendship had crossed a line into something else, Tracie's possessiveness grew. She acted as if she owned Paul.

Jennifer never brought up the disloyalty with Tracie, never talked about it or cleared the air. She let the mess pulse there like an open wound. It bled and grew every time she saw them together—which Tracie seemed to make sure happened all the time—and never healed.

Even now, Jennifer watched Tracie hang all over Paul while their host, poor Ed, stood there pining for her. Jennifer knew what a man in love looked like. She'd seen it on Paul's face often enough, and even now caught flashes from him aimed in her direction.

She saw it when Ed stood close to Tracie and tried to engage her in conversation. Ed wanted Tracie. Having nine friends crowded around him, all talking and fighting for attention, didn't change that fact.

Tracie was clueless. Jennifer added that flaw to the long list she'd mentally compiled on her former friend.

The one consolation was that Paul treated Tracie the same as he always had. He was protective and friendly. He never touched her or even winked at her.

"Jennifer? Your turn." Ed held out his hand as he stood at the base of the ladder to the loft.

The crowd swelled around the piles of hay, and the din of laughter drowned out the music on the radio. Jennifer didn't hesitate to take the risk despite the nerves jumping around in her belly. She climbed up the rickety steps, ignoring the creaks under her feet. She'd worn jeans and sneakers and left her hair unbound.

When she got to the top, she stared down from the rafters. She craved the wild freedom that would come with flying through the air but worried, with her recent bad luck, she'd miss the soft landing and go splat against the wooden floor.

Her gaze slipped to the right side and met Paul's. He smiled, and her nerves vanished. She could let go and be fine.

The air blew past her and she fell—one second light and the next flopping into the crunchy hay. She squealed with delight. All fear disappeared. Now it was a matter of waiting her turn to try again.

They spent the afternoon playing in the barn and running through the cornfields like kids. They ate lunch on a blanket in the tall grass, then broke out the kayaks and explored the stream on the far side of the barn. The warm fall day called them outside and they stayed there. Even Tracie's presence couldn't ruin this one.

By three o'clock, Jennifer thought she would drop over. The sunshine and racing around stole her energy. When everyone returned to the barn for another round of hay jumping, she took a pass. She hovered by the door and took great pleasure in watching her friends dance and laugh.

Paul stepped up behind her. "Want to see something?"

The naughty tone made her laugh. "Now there's a line."

"True, but this is real and totally wholesome."

"From you?"

"Amazing, isn't it? But I can actually keep my mind off more interesting things now and then."

It felt good to joke with him again. Their conversations had been so stilted and short since that night she saw him on the couch with another woman.

Jennifer glanced at Tracie, but she was too busy swinging from a rope hanging over the hay to notice the quiet conversation taking place right near her.

Jennifer forgot about Tracie the second after she saw her. "I'm game."

With his hand on her elbow, Paul guided Jennifer to a flat area a few hundred feet from the barn. "Almost there."

"Where?"

"Look." He pointed at the dark, four-legged bundles climbing over each other and gnawing on the edge of the blanket. "Rottweiler puppies."

"Oh my god! They are adorable." She fell to her knees and let the furry sweeties pounce on her. She massaged their ears and conceded to a round of demanded belly rubs from the fuzzy creatures.

Paul stood over her with his hands on his hips. "I've always wanted one."

"You should absolutely get one."

"When life is more settled and I'm not traveling for work. I'd have to keep them locked up all day, and I hate that. They need to run and play."

Jennifer fell back on the grass and laughed as two puppies licked every inch of her face. "Save me!"

"You are outnumbered." The amusement came through Paul's voice loud and clear.

"Then help."

He dropped down beside her. When he reached over to pick up the runt of the litter, two others bounded on his lap. The humans rolled in the grass, unable to speak through the choking laughter as they played with the puppies.

In the sunshine, wrapped in the scent of freshly cut grass, Jennifer felt a shot of pure joy. With the unconditional love of the puppies to keep them company, Jennifer and Paul wrestled with and petted the furry little guys while the rest of the world fell away.

They didn't see or hear anyone else. The universe consisted of two people drowning in happiness.

The moment went on for what felt like hours. They reveled in the time together and the soft sweetness of the puppies. It wasn't until the sun started to fade on the horizon and Ed walked up to them that the spell was broken.

"I see you found our newest household members." Ed wrangled one of the furry boys and picked him up.

Jennifer sat up and rested a hand on Paul's knee as she leaned over to kiss the cute little puppy he was holding. "They are so sweet."

Ed lifted the little guy in his arms until they were face to face. "Spoiled."

Paul didn't take his eyes off the puppies. "They deserve it."

Ed snorted. "Want one?"

"Wish I could." Paul glanced at Jennifer and a warm smile lit his face. "Someday I'll be ready."

She nodded. "I think you will."

"How could you do this to me?" Tracie threw her sweatshirt at Paul.

He trapped it against his chest in a rough catch and stood there. She was screaming loud enough to bring his neighbors running. She didn't speak during the entire drive back from the farm. She sat in the back seat and let the conversation whirl around her. She didn't participate. Didn't even move.

He tried to drop her off at her place, but she insisted on coming to his. Listening was his first mistake. Once she hit the front door, she whipped her bag in a corner and launched into a rage-filled stream of accusations. She'd been yelling, asking questions and not waiting for answers, ever since.

"Calm down," he said, knowing he was wasting his words.

"Why should I?"

He put down the drink he'd just retrieved and stepped out of the kitchen. Being away from the knives and heavy pans seemed like a smart move. There were limited potential weapons in the family room and more room to duck.

"What is wrong with you?"

"What do you think?"

Paul knew, just as he knew this explosion hovered in their future. Tracie saw something that wasn't there. He'd tried to ignore it and push her off, all while maintaining their friendship. Some days that was harder than others. Today it proved impossible.

"I've clearly upset you," he said.

"Don't you dare sound reasonable. You don't get to be the stable one. Not after what you did."

They stood on opposite sides of the couch. He wondered if that was enough of a boundary to save him. "We enjoyed a few hours with some friends. That's why we went up there in the first place. I don't see the problem."

She screwed up her lips in a scowl filled with hate. "Don't try to weasel your way out of this. I saw you with Jennifer."

He'd figured that out from the silent treatment during the car ride home. He'd been so wrapped up in the perfect moment he failed to notice Tracie hovering nearby. He never wanted to hurt her, but he hadn't asked for her obsession. He certainly hadn't promised to stay away from Jennifer.

"We were playing with the dogs. It was innocent. But, really, it's none of your business."

Desperation clawed at him. No matter how much sadness she aimed at him, he needed to hold on to the memory of the afternoon. The barn and water had been a great time, but playing with those dogs meant everything. Seeing Jennifer that carefree reminded him of the girl he once knew. Of the woman who stole his heart years ago and still owned it.

Loving one woman while another built her unrealistic expectations around him sent guilt crashing over him. He hadn't cheated or even done anything to make Jennifer question his loyalty, but he felt as if he'd broken vows to both women.

He exhaled, trying to figure out the best way to diffuse the situation. "Tracie, don't do this."

"You are cheating on me."

"That doesn't make any sense. We're not together."

"Then try this. You still love Jennifer."

He couldn't deny it. Couldn't laugh it off. So he ignored it and plowed through. "We're friends. Hell, you're Jennifer's roommate. Do you want us to pretend we don't know each other?"

"I'd settle for you acting as if you don't want to be with her."

The words sat there for a second. He'd struggled so hard to spare Tracie's feelings on this and hide his own. Jennifer kept begging for that, and he had to comply to survive with some of his dignity intact. Still, the past bubbled up on him now and then.

He looked at Tracie, the woman who had always helped him and supported him, and fumbled with the right words. "You and I are not together. Not like that. We never will be. It can't happen."

He saw a flicker of something in her eyes, something he could not identify. For the first time since that one telling night, he realized how she acted might have less to do with him than he thought. "Is this about guilt?"

Tracie lifted her head as if she'd smelled something awful and needed to rise above it. "I do not feel guilty."

"Really? You're trying to date your friend's ex."

Tracie continued to hold her body stock still. "You would take Jennifer back in a second if she gave you the chance."

That was his shame. His weakness. "That's my business."

Tracie put her hands on the back of the couch and leaned in. "She dumped you."

He fought off that reality every day and didn't want to hear it now. "Yeah, thanks. I got that."

This time Tracie's shoulders fell and a small gasp escaped her throat. "How can you still feel something for her? After the way she left?"

"I'll always have a special place for Jennifer. We've known each other for years."

Tracie stepped up and grabbed his arms as if willing him to listen. She tried to shake him, but she wasn't strong enough to move him. "You've known me for almost as long."

He didn't want to allow the comparison of Tracie and Jennifer into his head. "It's not the same. I don't want to hurt you—"

"Too late." Tracie dropped her hands to the side. "I hate you right now."

"I'm sorry."

"Not good enough." She turned and stormed away.

Paul could only hope she didn't lead Jennifer to think something more had happened between them as payback for his stolen happiness feeding her pain.

Thirteen

The forgive and forget motto is overrated.
Ignore it.

—Grandma Gladys, The Duchess

"YOU'RE LEAVING," TRACIE SAID FROM THE DOORWAY a few months later.

Jennifer did not take even a second to look up from her suitcase. She'd been packing all day. Boxes sat around her room as she tried to figure out what to take and what to give away. "I found a place closer to work."

"Another house?"

"An apartment. It's less expensive, which makes sense since I'm traveling for the job these days."

"Really?"

"I just said so, didn't I?"

Jennifer didn't even try to be civil. They spoke about house stuff and nothing more. Jennifer couldn't stand to be near her former friend, and she sure didn't like the way Paul now acted when he came by. He didn't joke or laugh with her anymore—ever since that day on the farm, when they'd played with the puppies. Something had happened between him and Tracie

105

after he gave her a lift in his car. . . . and she didn't return home till the wee hours of the morning.

What that something was, Jennifer didn't know. She didn't have the right to ask Paul, and Tracie had never offered the information, but the dynamics in the atmosphere when the three of them shared breathing space had gone from bad to worse. The situation made Jennifer sick.

"You sure there's not another reason you're leaving?" Tracie asked.

Jennifer wadded up the sweater in her hands and threw it in her bag. "Like?"

"I don't know." Tracie stammered and stuttered.

"What are you asking me?" Jennifer flung open the top of her suitcase and began filling it. Fast. She couldn't leave soon enough.

"This is just sudden. That's all."

Not to Jennifer. She'd been planning the move out for months. She'd tried to see Tracie's perspective and push all the bad feelings deep down so she could bury them. It didn't work.

Seeing Tracie made Jennifer furious. If anything, the anger grew with each day instead of shrinking. Heather had the same reaction.

"I've been thinking of going for a long time," Jennifer said.

Tracie came the whole way into the room. She looked at the bed covered with clothes and magazines like she wanted to snuggle in and have a girl talk.

Jennifer wasn't having it. Those days were gone. She shoved her suitcase to the edge of the bed and blocked Tracie's path. The act was juvenile, but Jennifer didn't regret it. Things would be much worse if she actually unlocked her tongue and spewed all the horrible things bottled up inside her. Holding back was the only concession she could muster.

"You didn't really give me any notice. How long have you been planning the actual move?" Tracie asked in a small voice.

Jennifer almost said the exact date but passed on the opportunity. "Months."

"We're not going to see much of each other after you go."

That was the idea. "Real friends stay in touch. It's a loyalty thing," Jennifer said with her coldest smile.

The shot would be as close as Jennifer got to telling Tracie off. She'd vowed not to whine or beg, but she made an exception for this tiny piece of passive-aggressive behavior.

Tracie stared at her nails. "And Heather is leaving."

"In a few weeks."

"So it's just me."

"You could always ask Paul to move in." Jennifer almost choked on the sentence. The idea of him moving in and playing house with Tracie made the blood rush out of Jennifer's head.

"It's not like that."

Good for Paul.

Jennifer didn't care about Tracie's problems. She created the situation and could live with it. "You can always get a roommate."

Tracie reached out her hand but stopped short of pressing hand to hand. "Jennifer . . ."

She moved out of touching range. "What?"

Tracie's body shrank in on itself. "Nothing."

Jennifer thought the word summed up the state of their relationship really well. "That's right. Nothing."

A year passed before she heard from Paul again. They knew many of the same people and would wind up across the room at parties, but Jennifer tried to limit those contacts. Being near him made leaving again all that much harder.

When she heard his name on the other end of the phone this morning, a thrill moved through her. When he asked if they could meet downtown for a walk at lunch, she couldn't say no. Despite everything, regardless of the wall she erected between them and continued to reinforce, she missed him.

She walked down the path with her coat wrapped around her and belted at the waist. The morning rain had broken open into a bright blue sky. Her heels clicked against the pavement as she approached the bench where they agreed to meet.

Even from a good distance away, she saw him. The sunshine lit his tawny hair. He'd clipped it shorter in a professional style that spoke to a grown-up job. He wore khakis and a blue sweater. The casual outfit suited him. He managed to look classy and sexy without being overdone.

As she moved closer, his head shot up and a warm smile burst across his lips. By the time she got to his side, he was on his feet. For a second she had a flash of the boy he'd been. The charm lingered there, but so did something else. A maturity and comfort she hadn't seen before.

He held her hand and leaned in to kiss her on the cheek. "You look good. Always do."

"And you can still sweet talk any woman you want."

He held his body different from before. She noticed the change right away. When they sat down and he stretched his arm behind her on the bench and his legs out in front of him, he did it with a practiced ease.

"I was surprised you called," she said as her gaze did a loving sweep of his face.

"Seemed like it was time."

"Why now?"

"Things would happen in my life and I'd pick up the phone to call you and then hesitate."

"There was nothing stopping you."

He exhaled. "I didn't like the way things ended."

She hated that part, too. Losing the close relationship she thought she had with Tracie and all those years of investment and intimacy was bad enough. Walking away from him and breaking what connection remained broke her heart.

"Me either," she whispered when her throat threatened to close.

"Thought we could see each other, enjoy an hour without all the other distractions and old arguments."

"That's a good plan." A group of young men hollered and cheered while they threw a ball around in the field to their right, but she could hear Paul just fine. "How's Tracie?"

Paul glanced at his watch. "It took you three minutes longer than I thought it would to mention her."

"Can you blame me?"

"Actually, no."

He looked at her then, all teasing gone.

"We were never together, Jennifer. What you saw on the couch that day—"

"Was none of my business."

His fingers tapped against the bench behind her. "Yet what you think you saw then is between us even now."

A huge ball of regret landed in her stomach. Amazing how a little conversation could shift everything into perspective. For weeks, she'd insisted to Heather that only Tracie was to blame. Now Jennifer realized she'd spread the blame evenly between Tracie and Paul, and it did him a disservice.

"It really doesn't matter anymore." She had to clear her throat twice to get the words out.

He rolled his eyes. "Oh, that's convincing."

"I guess Tracie keeps trying to make whatever you feel for her into something bigger."

Paul waited until Jennifer glanced his way again to speak. "It will never happen."

Jennifer went ahead and asked the question she'd been dying to ask. "Why?"

"First, I'm not interested."

"Oh." Jennifer hated how happy the information made her. "Is there another number?"

"And, two." He touched her hair briefly before pulling his hand away again. "You deserve to be treated better than that."

The silence thumped between them for a second too long before she spoke. "This doesn't have anything to do with me."

"Yeah, you keep thinking that." He squinted into the sun before looking at her again. "You still event planning?"

"I'm impressed you remember." That Paul could hold onto that piece of information after all this time made her ridiculously happy. She could feel the light spill through her.

"There isn't much about you that I forget."

"I'll take that as a compliment."

"That's how I meant it. I'm moving," he blurted out.

"Anywhere interesting?"

"Into the warehouse district."

The news made perfect sense. Artists lived there and worked there. No doubt Paul's outward calm radiated from an inner sense of peace for finding a place where he naturally belonged.

"That's great," she said.

He shrugged. "Yeah, I picked up a photography hobby and am playing in a band. Serious this time. We have some gigs."

"Drums?"

He scoffed. "Of course."

He'd expanded his hobbies and made them important in his life. He had a job and interests. He deserved all of the good turns. He was the very definition of a self-made man. But she couldn't help but feel left behind.

She held her body still and kept her voice steady as her insides shrank to a hollowed-out shell. "Not a surprise. You were destined to play the drums."

"I have a studio space and will be bunking there. Some big bands use the facilities, so I get experience and meet great people. It should be good."

Suddenly he was living the dream she craved, and he was doing it without her. One day soon he'd have someone else. He was too handsome and special to be alone for long. Maybe Tracie hadn't caught his attention, but some woman would.

Even though she'd loathed the idea, Jennifer had expected Paul and Tracie to get together. She figured Tracie would wear him down. But Paul's newfound life would threaten any chance Tracie ever had. She needed stability and a little house and a guy who went to a stable job and came home every night. A relationship where she was in charge and everything revolved around her.

The old Paul might have accepted that. The new version in front of Jennifer appeared to want more. He was embracing a new, full life, and she was so happy for him.

It also devastated her. She sat there smiling and enjoying the sound of his voice but had to fight the urge every minute to touch

him. A part of her wanted nothing more than to fall into the same
old pattern and have him love her again.

The only thing holding her back was the reality that walking
back into something with Paul had to be when—and if—they
were both ready and available. This still wasn't their time. He'd
found a life and she continued to search.

"You should come hear me play sometime. I'll even spring for
a drink." He winked.

"That's impressive."

"I'm a giving guy."

"Tracie would love to walk in and see me sitting there with
you." A dig, but one she couldn't resist.

His smile faded. "I'm asking you, not her. Besides, she doesn't
get a say. Whether she likes it or not, Tracie and I are friends.
Nothing more."

The reassurance allowed her to feel a little more charitable. At
least when it came to accepting that Paul didn't let friendships go
easily—and that included the years he had invested with Tracie.
She had been good to Paul. *Too* good.

"Are *we* still friends?"

"I'd like to think so, which is why I mentioned coming to hear
me play." He pressed his shoulder against hers, all playful and
full of the youthful boy she remembered. "Friends do that sort of
thing, you know."

"Maybe I will." But she wouldn't. They both knew she was being
polite. To save her sanity and the uncomfortable distance they
had built between them, she wouldn't. Couldn't. A breach would
lead them back down a road that sputtered to a dead end.

"I hope you do," he said with that smile that knocked her
breathless.

I miss you. The words were in her mouth, but she bit them back. "I'm happy for you."

He closed one eye and stared at her. "Why?"

"You seem to have your life together."

"I'm trying."

She laid her hand on his knee and savored the warmth of his skin through his pants. Muscles jumped beneath her fingers. "Let's keep in touch this time."

He slid his fingers through hers and held on. "We will."

"Promise?"

"Yeah."

They sat in silence for another fifteen minutes.

Fourteen

There are men who look good and men who are good.
Make sure you know the difference.

—Grandma Gladys, The Duchess

"I THOUGHT YOU WERE GOING TO MEET ME OUTSIDE."
Jennifer walked up to her sister's desk at her office. She dangled
the car keys in front of Heather's face. "What is taking so long?
We need to go."

It was Easter weekend and the plan was to head out early and
go to the cottage Jennifer had just bought on Lake Orr. An hour
and a half north of Toronto, her little slice of heaven sat on a
wooded piece of land that sloped right to the water. The interior
was an open design with a king-size bedroom, a loft and a Jacuzzi
that kept calling her name.

She wanted to hike and relax and watch the water. Heather's
tardiness made that impossible. She was moving folders around
on her desk and generally not getting her butt in gear.

"We'll go in a second."

"You're ticking me off." Actually, Jennifer had passed that point
as she sat in the car in front of the office building, waiting for her
sister to come outside.

"There's someone I want you to meet."

Jennifer rolled her eyes. Usually she could sniff out these match-making plans before they hatched and squash them. "Not even a little interested."

The guy she'd been dating lived in San Francisco. Not exactly the ideal distance for a relationship. He traveled, and their paths crossed infrequently. It hadn't been all that serious, but she still felt neglected. Breaking up hadn't been hard or messy. In some ways, that's what had her frustrated. She wanted to care enough to have the end matter. So far that had only happened one time in her life, and she still had trouble living with her decision over Paul.

"You need some fun." Heather eyed Jennifer's shirt as she spoke.

She glanced at her trim red turtleneck and black pants and saw business professional instead of party girl. "I'm fun."

"When?" Heather glanced behind Jennifer. "You're twenty-eight, not dead."

"I'm not debating that, but I want to get out of here. You might also remember that the last time you fixed me up it didn't go so well."

"If you're talking about Paul, you're wrong. You still love him, so I picked well. I can't be blamed for timing issues and unceasing fighting. You guys are responsible for those."

Two years had passed since Jennifer had seen him on a regular basis, and it still hurt to hear his name. She'd get a rare sighting on the street, but they hadn't talked since that day in the park.

She had to take responsibility for that one. He'd left the door open and she closed it, on purpose and with a sense of finality.

Heather shrugged. "This guy is different."

"Uh-huh."

"Funny and smart."

"So is Paul."

Heather threw open her arms and looked around in mock confusion. "Is Paul here?"

"No."

"This guy is."

"Not sure if I'm the 'this guy' in question, but I can pretend to be." The man with the deep voice and smile in his eyes moved next to the sisters.

Despite being angry with Heather and impatient to get home, Jennifer couldn't stop staring. There was something compelling about this one. The man had coal black hair and bright blue eyes. He was her romance fantasy look-alike come to life.

With his height soaring past six feet and the way he held his shoulders back and flashed that dimpled mouth, he could have walked off of the pages of a magazine. He reeked of power and self-assurance. Jennifer knew by looking at him that he drove an expensive car and knew his way around a wine bar.

And there was a bit of darkness behind those eyes. This one didn't always play by the rules. He likely took great pleasure in breaking them . . . as well as taking pleasure in a few other things. Yet he didn't come off as a jerk or know-it-all. He had the sophisticated male thing down.

"This is Preston." Heather turned to her sister and gave her a bug-eyed glare he couldn't see. "This is Jennifer."

"Hi, Jennifer." He shook her hand, holding on just long enough to forge a silent bond. "I've heard a lot about you."

She wanted to stay aloof and see how he reacted, but she blew that in the first few seconds. "Really?"

"Apparently you're perfect for me." He said it with enough suffered amusement to make Jennifer laugh.

She played along. "And I hear I will adore you."

"Aren't we the lucky ones?"

Yeah, charming. "Sounds like we could be."

"May I walk you ladies to your car?" He held out his arm for them to lead the way. "Wouldn't want you to be attacked by a horde of rampaging Easter bunnies."

His joking wiped out her grumpiness. "Is that a problem in this part of town?"

"Everywhere, actually. Very serious stuff." He winked at her before stepping ahead to hit the elevator button. "Would you two like to go down with me?"

Jennifer burst into laughter as she fell into the elevator car. "Wow."

"I have better lines, but you caught me off guard. I promise to work on that."

They slipped inside and stood side by side at the back of the elevator. Their shoulders touched, and Heather smiled from a safe distance at the front of the car.

"Off guard?" Jennifer asked.

"Heather kept telling me you were pretty and smart and lovely."

Jennifer shot her sister a smile. Maybe she'd let Heather live after all. "And?"

"You should have heard the description. Quite unbelievable. Frankly, I worried she was lying." He tipped his head toward Jennifer's. "Now I know she wasn't."

"What do you do?"

"Am I being tested?" Preston looked back and forth between them. "This sounds like a woman thing."

Jennifer let that go and skipped ahead to her question. "I'm just trying to figure out what a guy who throws out lines like that does for a living."

"I'd like to say something clever like power broker, but the real answer is contract specialist. I put together talent with companies who need it."

"That's how we met," Heather said. "Preston has been assembling a marketing team for my office."

"Interesting," Jennifer said.

His eyebrow shot up. "Is it?"

Jennifer burst out laughing. "I'm actually not sure."

They walked out of the lobby and to the car, talking about work and mindless stuff along the way. When he got to the driver's side, he crouched down on his haunches and peeked under the car.

Jennifer glanced at her sister and saw confusion. That made two of them. Jennifer gave in to the urge to ask. "What are you doing?"

His eyes narrowed with serious intent. "Checking for those killer bunnies."

The delivery was so dead-on perfect that the laughter bubbled up inside her and spilled out again before Jennifer knew what was happening. Heather gave a snort, too.

"I see," Jennifer said when she finally found control again. She knew right then she was going to have to give in on this one. "Are we safe then?"

"For now. But I can't promise you'll be safe at dinner."

She appreciated both the smooth style and his ability to get right to the point. "Ah, dinner."

"Since the attack has been thwarted, I'll go ahead and get in the car." Heather pointed to the door, and when no one tried to stop her, she climbed in.

"I'm assuming you do eat dinner every now and then." Preston leaned against the driver side, blocking Jennifer's way if she wanted to climb in.

She suddenly didn't. "Sometimes, yes."

"Any chance I can convince you to try a meal with me? This evening, maybe?"

She flipped her hair back over her shoulder and tried to remember the last time she made that move. "I have plans this weekend."

He winced. "Another man beat me to the question, I guess."

"I'm going away with Heather."

"That sounds more promising . . . for my future dinner plans with you, I mean."

"I'll be back on Monday."

He nodded to her. "Then I'll call you on Monday."

When he turned away, she called him back. "Don't you want my number?"

He winked. "Oh, I have it."

Paul's band had just finished its last set. He was hot and sweaty and completely invigorated. A little past 1:00 AM and the pounding beat and swell of the music still played in his head.

The guys had brought it home tonight. Under the lights with the crowd electrified, they'd done it. People sang along, danced and swayed. It was a dream come true even if it was a side job, one he did for the pure enjoyment of it rather than the need for an extra paycheck.

Paul downed half of his beer before he saw the woman sitting next to him at the bar. He smiled. She smiled back. He was growing accustomed to the musician's side benefit of female attention. Something about being up on that stage and playing drums acted like a magnet to women.

After almost every set he got an offer for action. A guy could learn to like the groupie scene.

He hadn't had a serious steady since Jennifer. And despite Tracie's attachment, when he moved into the warehouse district she was furious, like he betrayed her in some way, and she stopped talking to him. So he didn't have her in his life either.

Truth was, he had never been fair to Tracie. He said no to the idea of being a couple, but he accepted her friendship to hold off the boredom. It would have been fairer to put distance between them and let her move on since nothing was ever going to happen there.

Looked like he was one of those guys who gave his heart once and never again. If true, he'd used up his one shot with Jennifer. The one who got away and stayed there.

"Can I buy you another?" The woman touched his hand as she spoke. "I'm sure you've worked up quite a thirst."

He really looked at her then. Petite with long blonde hair and big brown eyes. She was more than pretty. She hovered in the knock-out range. He couldn't make out that much of her since she was sitting on a barstool, but the slim jeans and enticing shadow between her breasts, just where the neckline dipped low, told him the body matched the face.

From his experience, pretty meant tough to handle. Sometimes it meant crazy. He'd spent three weeks with an aspiring actress and never knew which personality would open the door when he knocked. No way was he going down insanity alley again.

"I'm Paul." He held out his hand, and she slid hers inside.

"Wendy."

He refrained from picking up every cute music fan who crossed his path. Being the guy a woman wanted to try on the side or when drunk or just when she wanted to try a musician wasn't really his thing.

But he wasn't dumb enough to turn down a sure thing who happened to be really hot. "You like music, Wendy?"

"I like yours." She twirled her glass, letting the brown liquid dance. "Do you play at other places?"

"Why?"

"I might want to see you again." She crossed her legs.

The move had his gaze traveling all over her. He tried to be subtle but realized he'd failed when she sent him a sexy I'm-yours-anytime smile.

A smile he wanted to see again. "We can meet up somewhere else or you can continue to see me right now."

"That sounds good."

"Which part?"

"All of it."

He liked her style. Blunt and self-confident. Those were pretty sexy traits in a woman.

"Do you have a preference?" Wendy asked.

He needed a shower and a good night's sleep. Being alone was the smart way to go. Heading out was the responsible thing to do. *Screw that.*

She made her intentions clear. So would he. "Want to get a table? We can talk for awhile."

"Is that what you really want to do, Paul?"

The green light flashed in front of him. "No, but I was trying to be a gentleman."

"I'm impressed."

The exhaustion left his bones. The inevitable crash that came hours after pouring everything into the music didn't threaten to overtake him. As the minutes ticked by, he got more keyed up not less.

That could only mean one thing. This lady was doing some-thing for him. Something he wasn't about to ignore. "But I'd be just as happy to talk back at your place."

Her gaze toured his face. Whatever she saw must have worked for her because she dragged a pen out of her purse and jotted down a few lines on her drink napkin. "I'll meet you there in ten minutes."

"We can share a ride."

She slipped off the barstool. "A smart woman doesn't leave her car behind."

And a smart man didn't question his luck. "I'll be in your drive-way by the time you open the door."

Fifteen

Not every relationship has to be forever
but be sure to know the difference.

—Grandma Gladys, The Duchess

PRESTON HANDED THE MENU TO THE WAITER. "SHE'LL have the fish."

Jennifer lowered her napkin to her lap and stared across the white linen to the other side of the table. She waited until the waiter left the table to say anything. "I was thinking of a steak."

"Too heavy."

"Me or the meat?"

"You'll love the fish." Preston smiled at her over the top of his wine glass. "Trust me."

"This isn't really a trust issue."

He winked at her. "Wouldn't you rather talk about something else?"

"I'd rather have the steak," she muttered at his dismissal.

"Jennifer," he said in that warning tone that made her jaw snap shut.

"What?"

"We are in this beautiful restaurant on this lovely night." He reached across the table and folded her hand in his. His thumb traced her knuckles as his voice slipped into husky territory. "Surely we can think about other things to discuss."

She tried to block out the warning bells ringing in her ears. "Like what?"

He pulled his hand back. "Anything would be preferable."

"Of course."

But she couldn't block out the growing tentacles of dread. They wrapped around her and squeezed until she couldn't breathe.

At first she'd thought his habit of ordering for her was sexy, kind of chivalrous. It showed off his knowledge of wines and love of food. After an unending menu of fish and salad, she wondered if something else was at play.

She'd lost more than ten pounds since they started dating. She wasn't dieting, but he seemed to be monitoring and guiding her food choices.

She hated that.

She glanced around the upscale restaurant. All the men wore expensive suits and sat with women clad in elegant black dresses. They gave off an air of careful perfection. She sensed it hid a chilling cold inside.

Silverware clanked and almost none of the couples engaged in conversation. It was as if the universe threw together a bunch of random, well-dressed strangers and forced them to sit down to eat. No matter how hard she tried, Jennifer couldn't pick out a single twinge of warmth in the room.

Her gaze wandered to Preston as he signaled for the waiter. Their clothes mirrored everyone else's seated at the round tables outlining the room's central fireplace. At least on the outside. Underneath, she wore the lacy matching underwear and thighhighs he'd purchased for her and laid out on the bed as she showered.

After only ten months he'd fallen into the habit of picking out her underwear and her food. It made her worry about what he'd try to control by the time they hit the twelve-month mark. If they even made it that far.

Some days she wanted to end it. Others, the relationship fed her like a drug.

"I found a place." She dropped the conversation nugget even knowing it could touch off a prickly debate.

He froze in the act of swirling his wine. "When?"

"This afternoon."

He blinked twice. "On your own?"

Sometimes he acted like she needed a chaperone to go to the bathroom. Never mind that she had a college degree and high-powered job. "My apartment lease is up."

"Yes, I understand that."

"Well, I couldn't wait any longer. I didn't have a choice." Never mind the fact she snuck away to handle it without him. It was cowardly and dumb, but she didn't want the hassle. Picking an apartment was personal and shouldn't require a verbal battle.

"We talked about this."

"No, you talked about this."

He frowned at her before waving the poor requested waiter away from their table. "Why are you acting like a child?"

"You mean, like I have a brain." She couldn't stop pushing him, despite the rage she saw burning in his eyes.

"Is now really the time for this?"

She glanced at the table next to theirs and saw a fifty-something woman staring back. "I guess not," she mumbled.

"Exactly. There's no reason for us not to move in together."

She knew he would keep at it until she caved. That was their pattern. She held firm, he poked, and she gave in out of pure exhaustion. Sometimes it was just easier not to argue.

But she tried anyway. "I'm not ready."

"That is ridiculous."

"Why?"

He broke his rule and put his elbows on the table. The move allowed him to stretch across the table and lean in closer. "We already spend every evening together."

"Not quite."

His eyes narrowed. "Why are you afraid?"

Because she wasn't dumb. "I'm not."

"Listen." He held his hand to his ear. "Do you hear it?"

"What?"

"The patter of feet."

"*What?*"

"You're running scared."

Jennifer glared at the woman seated next to them, who was making no attempt to hide her annoying eavesdropping. The lady nearly slid off her chair and fell to the floor while trying to listen in.

Jennifer dropped her voice lower to see if the other woman would climb up on the table to keep up with the conversation. "I just want to remain independent."

Preston laughed. "Isn't it too late for that?"

"What is that supposed to mean?" Jennifer didn't even try to hide her anger that time. The volume of her voice climbed until the other woman's dinner companion joined in the staring.

"We're together," he said.

"And we can be together with separate apartments. We've done it so far and have done fine."

"But imagine what we could accomplish from the same apartment."

Jennifer thought about some of their late-night adventures and flopped back in her chair. "Nothing legal, I imagine."

The waiter set the salad down in front of her. The sudden urge for a creamy soup overwhelmed her. She thought about shoving the fennel aside and ordering what she wanted.

Only the sexy smile on Preston's lips stopped her. "If we eat really fast we can find something better to do this evening." He leaned over to their unwanted eavesdroppers. "Maybe you ladies would care to join us?"

They sputtered. One pressed her hand against her chest as if to ward off an impending heart attack.

"I was thinking we'd try one of those swingers' clubs." His smile never wavered as he looked from one lady to the other. "Interested, ladies?"

They pulled away fast enough to move their table sideways and a foot in the opposite direction.

"Well, that's unfortunate," he said in his most proper voice.

Jennifer watched it all with a hand slapped across her mouth. It was either that or fall over laughing. The scene was so typically Preston. He controlled his surroundings and always had that one droll comment that would break through her frustration and wipe out all the bad stuff.

Preston sat straight in his chair again and smiled at Jennifer. "Looks like it's just us."

She bit her bottom lip. "Guess so."

He moved the lettuce around with his fork. "That's a shame. We could have given them something to tell their friends."

"I think you just did."

"Are you going to marry her?"

Paul stood on the boat's deck and watched the other members of the dive plunge into the frigid Atlantic Ocean. He conducted a final test on his mask while Neil talked.

Keeping up with the conversation proved tough, but Paul picked out the word marriage and knew this wasn't a topic he cared all that much about. "Who?"

"Who do you think I'm talking about?" Neil grabbed onto the rail when the boat rocked beneath them. "Wendy."

"We're about to check out a scuttled ship, one of the best dive sites off Nova Scotia, and you're talking about my love life?"

"Just asking a question."

"I'd rather focus on the HMCS *Saguenay* right now." Paul glanced over the side but couldn't see anything more than the other divers in the water. The sky was a bright blue but the air was cool.

And he wanted to concentrate on the Atlantic and everything lurking in the water underneath them.

They'd flown almost two hours to Lunenburg and paid a decent fee to get places on this tour. Through all of that, he hadn't given Wendy a thought. He knew that was wrong, but it's how his mind worked. He was focused on this dream vacation. It was all that mattered.

"Besides, it hasn't even been a year yet." It was the same argument Paul used when Wendy dropped a hint the week before.

Truth was, he didn't plan on marrying anyone. He'd given everything to a woman who walked out on him . . . repeatedly. He was older now but little had changed. He'd tried to work up the same level of feeling for Wendy and a line of women before her, all without success.

He was beginning to think that the depth he experienced with Jennifer happened once, and if you didn't grab it, you lost it. From there, you were doomed to achieve *almost* but no more.

"Is there a time limit for these things with women? Seems to me they start thinking about weddings and other crap the second they decide you're good enough to sleep with," Neil said.

"You been hanging out with a lot of women lately?"

"Not as many as I want."

"Now that I can understand." Paul took his position next to the open railing at the side of the boat. He was ready to put land and this conversation behind him.

"She mentioned it, you know."

Paul's head shot up. "What?"

"You heard me."

The guy waiting to go after them shifted his weight around. "Uh, I thought you two wanted to dive today."

Neil waved the other man off and focused on Paul. "Wendy told Sharon you were the one."

Paul shuffled to the side so the guy could take a turn with the instructor's help. "When?"

"At the party last week. Brian heard it, too."

Paul shook his head. Leave it to his roommate to keep a big thing like that quiet. Thanks, Brian. And thanks to Sharon, Neil's girlfriend, for gossiping to Neil and otherwise making Paul's dive miserable. "Brian never mentioned it."

"This is more of a chick thing," Neil said.

"Then why are we talking about it?"

Neil grew more serious. "Consider it a warning."

"Meaning?"

"I know you're still hung up on Jennifer."

"That's long over." Paul could finally say the words without doubling over.

For years he refused to think them, let alone speak them. Now he could talk the talk without feeling anything. The reality of losing her numbed him to everything else.

"If you say so."

"Can we dive now?" Paul got back into position.

"Just know that I'll say 'I told you so' when the time comes and Wendy starts making demands."

Paul planned to push that day off as long as possible. "Keep this up and I'll drown you while we're down there."

"Fair enough."

Three years passed before Jennifer could catch up with everything happening around her. She was facing another end of a lease and increased pressure from Preston to move in together.

His hands fell on her shoulders and gently shifted her position until she looked out the ten-foot windows of the warehouse loft. "My friend was right about this place."

Preston got a lead about the loft but was told they had to move fast if they wanted it. As usual, Preston's connections led her to something she'd only heard or dreamed about.

"It's amazing." She'd never been so impressed by a thing before.

Her usual taste ran to cozy cottages. This place oozed character and cried out for nightly parties. The neighbors were businesses who shut their doors at the end of every business day. Here they would have privacy and not have to worry about making too much noise or irritating the people downstairs.

The set designer who last rented the apartment updated the kitchen and laid out every inch to perfection. The place was about a thousand square feet with soaring twenty-foot ceilings. The walls were painted a soothing color and the furniture arranged to highlight the bright light and dramatic view.

Jennifer wanted it the moment she saw it.

"It's perfect for us," he said.

"What's the rent?" When Preston told her, she blew out a disappointed breath. "No way."

"What?"

"That's way too expensive." She'd have to cut out everything including the utilities to swing it, and that level of deprivation didn't do anything for her. It wasn't practical. She wasn't even sure it was possible on her salary, even with reasonable expenses and low debt.

"There's a solution." He turned her around in his arms until her gaze met his.

She knew what he was about to say and cut off the mantra before he could chant it. "I know what you're going to say."

"And?"

"Honestly?"

"Of course."

"I promised myself I'd never live with a man."

She believed in her heart that sort of commitment meant marriage and children, and she didn't see either with Preston. Ever. He was fun and wild and took her into the life she'd known as out there, just beyond her reach. With him, she could have all that. Everything except a real future.

"I'm thinking we've done a lot of things together you never thought you'd do. Probably a few you didn't imagine were possible. What's this one final step?"

She felt the heat hit her cheeks at the subtle reminder of some of the more out-there parties he'd taken her to. "I know you don't think so, but there are some parts of me that are very conventional."

"You're not in Sarnia anymore, Jennifer."

"What is that supposed to mean?" But she knew. He'd said the words often enough for her to know how little he thought of her life before him.

"You left there to escape your sheltered existence."

"That's not—"

"You walked away from the safe road a long time ago." He cupped her cheek as his thumb brushed over her lips. "You were strong."

"I am strong."

"But now you see something you want and you're backing away." He placed a quick kiss on her lips. "I want to know why."

"It's a lot of money."

"You're making up problems. Together we can swing it." His blue-eyed gaze lasered in on her.

She felt the heat and determination run through every part of him. He vibrated with the need to win her over. To convince her and reel her in.

"You once told me you wanted a life that was more exciting than your dreams." He wrapped an arm around her shoulders and pulled her tight to his side.

"True." Her gaze followed his arm as he swept around the large space.

"You can have everything you want. All you have to do is open your mind and take the step. Say yes."

She took in the windows and the the shiny floors. Saw the potential and ignored the realities. "Yes."

His hold tightened. "Good girl."

Sixteen

There is a wild side in you that's dying to get out.
Give it air and room to breathe.

—Grandma Gladys, The Duchess

"It's a party, not a funeral. Of course, it's a goth party, so you could technically call it both." Preston looked in the full-length mirror attached to their bedroom wall and ran his fingers through his perfect hair.

Jennifer wanted to kick him with her black stiletto boots. Ten minutes ago, he threw half of her clothes on the floor and declared them matronly. Now he joked as if nothing had ever happened.

Maybe she should kick him twice.

He finally stopped looking at his reflection and stared at her through the mirror. His mouth was flat and his expression unreadable. "What? Are you actually pouting?"

She couldn't stop shaking long enough to make a face. She'd lost control of her limbs and didn't know if it was due to fear or fury.

Four months into living together and he had morphed into a man who wanted to control her in every way. Oh, he still charmed her and those around her, but the other side of him snuck out more regularly now. The part of him that demanded complete allegiance.

"I am a grown woman. I can pick my own clothes."

He rolled his eyes. Even threw in one of his you're-an-idiot snorts. "That's debatable."

She ignored the verbal and visual smack down. "I know how I want to look."

He held up his hand. "That's enough."

"Excuse me?"

"The conversation is tiresome."

Kicking no longer seemed sufficient. "So is your attitude."

"You're acting like a petulant child."

"According to you." She yelped when he turned around and leaned over her on the bed. Caging and trapping her until the need for flight burned up her throat. "What are you doing?"

One minute she sat with her legs hanging over the side and her body wrapped in a towel. The next she was dangling naked in his arms.

He treated her to a cold smile. "I was merely making a suggestion about your wardrobe. Stop acting like it's something more."

"You issued a command."

He lowered her back to the ground and brushed his hand down the back of her cheek. "So dramatic."

"I didn't—"

He pressed a finger against her lips. "You like when I take over."

"No." What started as exciting had slowly gotten stranger. The dark side of his personality seeped into every aspect of their lives. Nothing was off limits to him.

But she couldn't blame Preston for showing her parts of the city and a nightlife she knew existed but had never seen. She went willingly just to satisfy her nosy gene. The life fed her curiosity and need for a world outside the one she'd known back in Sarnia.

"Is it so bad that I want you to be beautiful?" He pulled her hair up and balanced it on top of her head as if assessing whether he liked the look.

If he noticed she was naked, he didn't show it. His focus centered on his hair creation, as if only the part of her he controlled mattered.

"I'd like to think I'm pretty no matter what I'm wearing." She bent her knees and grabbed a shirt off her bed. She held it to her chest, letting it drape over the rest of her. "You used to think I was."

"Stop being so sensitive." He let her hair fall back against her face. "Are you going to wear a wig?"

"I don't know."

"You should."

In honor of her grandmother, she dyed her hair black and wore it long and straight. Every photo of the Duchess showed off that style. Jennifer loved it. She thought it worked well on her by highlighting her eyes and flattering her skin tone.

Preston hated it.

He preferred the more extreme looks. Even now he went to a chest under her window and opened the lid to paw through her wig collection. He threw a platinum blonde one on the bed. "Wear this."

"I'm fine with my own hair tonight."

He exhaled, filling the sound with a stifling load of disappointment. "You are still so closed off. Even after all this time your experience is limited. You need to open yourself up to something wild."

He'd made the insinuation before. "Like?"

"There are things I can show you."

They went out all the time. Preston was not the type to sit around watching a hockey game or joking with friends over a beer. There was no such thing as a quiet night at home with Preston. He wanted action all the time. At first, she found that intoxicating. Now it exhausted her.

"It's all in here." He pressed his hand against her heart, less as a loving gesture than a claim of ownership. "I can feel it."

She pulled out of his grasp. "Preston, don't."

"We just need to dress you up, let you be someone else for a few hours so you can let go."

"I can be whoever I want."

He snapped his fingers. "What was the name you used the other night when we went out?"

"Victoria Sinclair."

The more her real life diverged from this one, the more she felt like two people. Office worker Jennifer would never stay out all night and ignore her obligations. Victoria welcomed the wild life. As Victoria, she could banish the shyness and explore. Like the wigs and clothes, the name was part of a persona that let her walk into the world as someone else.

"Victoria." Preston said the name like he was tasting it. "Very good. It suits you."

She hated that he liked Victoria more than Jennifer. To her, they were sides of the same woman. To him, it was a choice and he wanted only her Victoria half.

"It's an identity," she mumbled.

"One you should nurture."

That was her intent but knowing Preston's preference ruined it for her. "Maybe."

"I know what I'd like to see." He grabbed the bag he'd brought with him to the apartment.

"You bought an outfit for me."

"I know what I want."

"What about what I want?"

"That's irrelevant tonight." He opened her hand and put the bag in it. "Trust me."

An hour later they rode in a rickety elevator in an old fabric warehouse that now housed half of the city's underground goth movement. The walls were sickly green and the space cramped. She hadn't said two words to Preston since he rushed her out of the apartment in the outfit he bought and deep red lipstick.

Even now she stood there seething, wondering why she'd let him boss her around. She was about to unleash when a gentleman dressed in full vampire gear, complete with the cape and fake pointy teeth, stepped inside. At least Jennifer hoped they were fake. The man hovered by the number panel in stony silence.

He waited until the doors closed before turning around to face them. "I assume we're all going to the same place."

"The Greenberg wedding?" Preston's joke broke the tense silence in the car.

The vampire laughed, and so did she. By the time they stepped off the elevator and onto the floor of the party, she'd been wound up in his spell once more. She marveled at how he did it. One minute he could throw out a line that stunned everyone with his wit. The next he could break down her self-confidence and stomp her common sense to dust.

Preston appeared in front of her and delivered a deep bow. He held his arm out to her. "Madam, I believe they're playing our song."

She listened to the banging techno music shouting through the dark industrial space and smiled. She could barely hear, let alone dance. "Sounds like a waltz."

His smile was filled with satisfaction. "I knew you wouldn't back down."

She slid her arm through his. "Not yet."

"That's my Victoria."

"Another scuba diving trip?" Wendy stopped in the process of unloading the grocery bags. She had a gallon of milk in one hand and a cartoon of eggs in the other.

Paul waited for her to drop both. "There are six of us."

"How long will you be gone?"

He wanted her to put everything down before the conversation went much further. If he'd known that look of shock would move over her face at the news, he would have waited to share it until they were relaxing on the couch after dinner.

He'd been dreaming about this for a long time, before he met Wendy at the bar and certainly before they moved in together. He'd talked to her about his dream of hitting the best spots along the Atlantic coast.

From her reaction he assumed she never thought it would happen. She likely believed he would try it once and stop, but Lunenburg just fueled his desire to keep going. So much for believing in him.

"I'll be back in three weeks," he said.

"What about your job?"

He leaned against the refrigerator and watched her work. She went from still to constant motion. She wiped her hands on her jeans and raced around the kitchen putting everything away with Olympic speed.

"I travel six months a year for my work, then I get a break. You know how this works. You knew I had time coming and wanted to take a trip. It was just a matter of getting in with a planned dive in the right location and at the right price."

She tried to slam the refrigerator door but it closed with a soft bump. "I thought we'd spend the time together."

"You have to work."

"Excuse me?"

Admittedly, it was a lame excuse. He reached for anything in his brain and that one popped out. He regretted the lack of tact but not the content.

She'd moved in to the apartment he shared with Brian just months after meeting. Brian didn't complain because his share of the rent went down and there was always food in the house. Paul appreciated all the touches, but fought being swept up in it all.

She wanted a commitment and permanence. He wasn't ready to go there. It was too fast, and maybe it would never happen. He wanted it to. Hell, he really wanted it. She was beautiful and into him. But for the first time in his life he understood Jennifer's refrain in needing to grow on his own before committing to someone else.

"Wendy, cut me a break here. I've been wanting to try this forever. I have my certification. My gear."

"So?"

Not the easiest argument to fight but he tried. "I have the opportunity to try some amazing dive sites. I'm not going to miss that."

"What about me?"

"You'll be here."

"And?"

He had no idea what the right answer was to this obvious female test. "I go. I dive. I take some photos. I come back. This is not that difficult to understand."

"And you expect me to just wait."

He almost reminded her how she was the one who pushed them into living together. She put them on fast forward, not him. "It's three weeks, not three years."

"It's about making decisions together and if you don't get that . . ." She shook her head. "Forget it."

He knew he had to follow her to the bedroom.

He also knew he had to go on the dive.

Seventeen

Never lose yourself in a man.

—Grandma Gladys, The Duchess

HEATHER SLIPPED INTO THE DOORWAY. "YOU SUR you're okay?"

Jennifer stared in the bathroom mirror and concentrated on perfectly applying her lipstick. "Yeah."

"I'm your big sister. You can tell me anything."

"Like?"

"Preston."

"We're dating." She glanced at the small clock on the shelf above the towels. "And he'll be home in ten minutes, so I have to get moving."

"Heaven forbid you not be ready when the master comes through the door."

"What does that mean?"

Heather's head fell to the side against the door frame. "He's got you doing these things—"

"I don't do anything I don't want to do." Jennifer said the words but didn't believe them.

The pressure from Preston never stopped. He told her what to wear and what to eat. He tried to get her to switch banks and frequently paged through her checkbook. She'd found him more than once going through her purse and then claiming to be looking for something like gum.

And as intrusive as that stuff was, it was minor. His violent mood swings went from infrequent to the norm. He called her Victoria regularly now. More and more, in his eyes, Jennifer disappeared.

"Life is exciting with him. He knows everyone and is connected to this life I never knew existed." Jennifer repeated the excuse she told herself over and over.

"But seeing it and being in it are two different things."

"With him, I can be or do anything. The shy girl who works hard and follows the rules goes away." She could talk to people and fit in. The clothes put her in the place where the line between Victoria and Jennifer blurred.

"You're still her."

Jennifer put the lid on the lipstick and set it down on the sink. "Not when I'm Victoria Sinclair."

Heather's started to say something then stopped. It took a few seconds before she started again. "I don't understand why you can't just be you. Why isn't that good enough for him?"

Jennifer searched for the right explanation but couldn't mentally grab onto it. "Think about our lives. We grew up in a pretty isolated environment. Even now we hold down jobs and do what is expected of us."

"I get all that."

Jennifer held her sister's hands and willed her to listen. Really hear the need. "Now imagine that for a little while you could

break out and step into this world you'd never imagined. People are free and artistic and not tied down to the norm.

Heather squeezed Jennifer's fingers. "So is he the one?"

"For what?"

"Forever, Jennifer. Is he whatever you've been waiting for your whole life?"

Jennifer dropped her sister's hand and stepped back as far as the small room would allow. "No."

"Then I don't get it. Why waste the time?"

"Preston's not the guy you marry and have kids with. You have fun with him."

"That's all this is?"

"Yes."

"You're not building a future with him. This is some kind of holding pattern?"

Jennifer could see the worry and panic in Heather's face. It washed off of her and over Jennifer. "I'm just having fun."

The word sounded hollow even in her own ears. She tried to convince herself that life with Preston consisted of fun and excitement, but many times it revolved around something different. Around control and his silent demand of obedience. She felt disgusted by those parts.

"Okay." Heather turned around.

Sadness welled up in Jennifer. She called after her sister before she could disappear from sight. "I love you, you know."

"Same here." Heather's voice grew softer. "That's why I tried to talk to you."

"You should have worn the red dress instead of the black," Preston said as they walked into the crowded bar.

This place sat on a refurbished block in the warehouse district. The rooms were full, and cigarette smoke clogged the air. Jennifer couldn't see much through the crush of people, but she noticed one thing. This was not one of their usual hangouts.

This was the place people came and admitted they were there. No one dressed up or had sex in the hall by the bathroom. A normal bar.

"I like this dress," she said as she smoothed her hand over her ever-shrinking stomach.

"The other would have shown off your tiny waist. Since you've lost the weight and gotten so fit, you should show it off."

"Heather thinks it's too much." So did Jennifer. The constant workouts and liquid lunches were taking a toll. If she stood up too fast, she got dizzy.

"She should come out with us then, shouldn't she?" Preston nodded to the women milling around. "She'd realize super thin is the 'in' look."

"I'm not convinced I can keep it up."

"Sure you can."

Jennifer refused to have this fight, especially not in public. "Why are we here?"

"I thought we'd have a drink and then head to the real party."

"What does that mean?"

"Don't worry about it. I'll take care of our activities. You can just stand there and look pretty."

She took in his glassy eyes and heavier-than-usual hand and wondered what was going on. "Preston—"

"I need to meet with someone for a second."

There was nothing normal about this evening. "Who?"

"Have a seat at the bar."

He walked away as soon as he issued the order. She watched his broad back disappear into the throngs and pop up again by the door marked manager. She had no idea why they were here, but it wasn't just to take a look around. Preston moved in different circles than this.

She liked the bar. It felt comfortable and familiar. But it lacked his required level of style.

At the moment, she didn't exactly fit in either. She was over-dressed. The outfit showed off a good deal of leg. The red wig hid her Victoria side from her real-life, but she felt oddly out of place wearing it now.

"Jennifer?"

She froze. She'd know that voice anywhere. It played in her dreams and owned her memories. She turned and faced the man who once meant everything to her.

His green eyes wandered over her face. "That is you, right?"

"Hello, Paul."

The years had been good to him. He was tan and trim. Handsome with a sweet smile that still pinged her heart. He wore black pants and tee.

He fit in just right with this place. Better than he would have when they were together.

"I've never seen you here before." He rested his elbow on the bar and leaned in.

The closeness enveloped her, along with the clean scent of his skin. She knew he crowded her so they could hear over the steady hum of conversation from the people around her, but for a second she let herself believe this went deeper.

"I'm just making a quick stop." She shouted that fact right into his ear.

Paul took a quick glance around the bar. "Alone?"

"No."

He smiled. "Ah."

She looked at his hand and noted there was no ring. She'd heard through the gossip trail that he was living with a woman named Wendy. A woman who looked like Jennifer's exact opposite, which she found interesting.

"What's with the wig?" he asked.

"Just playing."

"I like your real hair." He lifted his hand as if he was going to touch there but then let it drop.

"People like to pretend." It felt like a childish and stupid game. Paul didn't appear to judge, but she measured her life by her time with him, and this period suddenly fell short.

"You've never had to be anyone other than who you are. Jennifer was always pretty special in my book."

Her heart melted a fraction. "How is it that, even after all this time, you know the exact right thing to say to knock me off guard?"

"I wonder why you think you'd need to be in battle stance around me in the first place."

She realized she didn't.

She ran her hand over the fake hair. In Preston's world, she dressed up and fit in. It all struck her as odd now. "I wanted to try something new."

"I can understand that."

"Have you? Tried anything new, I mean?"

"Just got back from a dive trip. Took up photography. Typical boring stuff."

It was honest and real. Everything about him was. "You are anything but boring."

She looked past Paul and saw Preston leave the manager's office and start through the crowd toward her. A stark desperation ran through her and settled in her stomach. She didn't want these two men to meet. Didn't want her world with Preston to taint her memories of Paul.

"I should go." She tried to act cool, but her movements were jerky and fast.

"It's okay."

She stopped glancing around, waiting for her worlds to collide, and focused on Paul. "What is?"

"Whatever has you so upset."

"I'm fine." She tried to walk past him and get to the door.

He stopped her with a gentle hand on her elbow and turned her back around to face him. "You sure?"

She was tired of people asking her that. She absolutely didn't want Paul to think her life was anything but great. "Of course."

"For the record? As hot as this look is, and it really is, I prefer the real you."

Her defensive shields raised. That fast, they snapped into place. "Maybe this is the real me."

Paul let her go. "And maybe not. Either way, I hope you figure it out."

Eighteen

Don't let fear keep you from getting what you need.

—Grandma Gladys, The Duchess

IT WAS 1999, AND SHE NO LONGER KNEW WHERE TIME went. So much had happened in the years since she met Preston. Some of it was good, most of it was exciting, but the dark times lingered in her memory as well.

The darkness receded as she watched him sit at the kitchen table with papers spread out in front of him, listening to whatever the man across from him was saying. Allan was a business associate. A guy who connected inventors with investors. Allan and Preston did business together, and Allan showed up today to talk about some big opportunity.

As Preston laughed at something Allan said, she wondered if there were two of him. The rational and fun side, the part that made her smile and challenged her to political discussions. Then there was the demanding, break-her-down side. The longer they were together, the more difficulty she had telling the sides apart.

He knew people everywhere and had his fingers in everything. He listened, watched, and waited. No matter how he treated her, he had this ability to charm even the hardest heart. With the right smile and a well-placed comment, he could part people with their money and make things happen.

He rolled with big players, enjoying drinking lunches as they discussed everything from banking to media. He talked with owners and investors, always on the lookout for an opportunity. People trusted him, and he returned their belief in him by making piles of money.

"Maybe Victoria would be interested," Allan said.

"Jennifer," she mumbled under her breath.

Preston held out his hand. "It's an interesting venture."

She went over to him because the outstretched arm suggested she better. "What is it?"

"You're not going to believe it." Preston tapped his pen as a look of smug satisfaction slid across his mouth. "An Internet start-up."

"You hear about one of those every week." She felt his heated scowl on her face, but she didn't back down. "The Internet is still new. It's all a gamble."

"Some hit."

She was challenging him in front of his business associate just for the sake of ticking him off, but she couldn't stop. "Many don't."

His jaw tightened. "This is different."

"Uh-huh."

"I need a woman. The right woman," Allan said.

Sounded ominous. "For what exactly?"

"A friend of a colleague, a guy named Walt, wants to deliver something so out there, so risky, it has to work." Allan's eyes gleamed with excitement. "A show where a woman would deliver the news and weather . . ."

So far she didn't hear anything original or worthy of the bright shine in his eyes and obvious thrill thrumming through the man. "Yeah?"

"While she strips."

Her brain shuddered to a halt. "Strips?"

Preston chuckled. "Gets naked. She tells the audience what's happening in the world while she takes her clothes off. It would be called Naked News."

Her breath refused to come for long enough that she wondered if her lungs had shut down. "A naked woman delivering the news."

Allan leaned across the table with all the energy of a little boy desperate go outside on a rainy day. "Right. This isn't just about showing off bodies or sterile photos in a magazine. We're talking live women broadcasted right into people's living rooms. No waiting. Men can hear their voices and see them. Appreciate them as real human beings."

It struck her as scary but brilliant. "But from a perspective of being smart. Not porn, but news."

Allan slapped the table. "Exactly! Women reporting the news as they strip."

"I'd watch it just to see how it would work." She admired any woman who would have the guts to try it.

She wasn't a prude. She viewed sex as healthy and normal and a woman's body as beautiful. But clothes provided protection. They separated her from the world and let her be whoever she wanted to be.

"It would be a subscription-only program, an add-on, until it gains an audience. The goal is for it to become self-supporting. We'd be looking for ways to grow viewership long-term." Allan ticked off the selling points as he shuffled through his papers.

The idea sounded so raw and appealing in her head. She loved the thought of women feeling comfortable with their bodies and celebrating their flaws instead of hiding them. Shedding inhibitions and presenting something new, in a way that no one had tried, was a perfect match for the Internet.

Where Preston fit in was her question. "What's your role?"

He held up his hands. "Just talking it through with Allan here."

Allan jumped in. "My job is to find a woman—the right woman—one who is smart and beautiful and more than a little adventurous. Someone who can command attention with both her body and her brain."

Jennifer tried to imagine who would take the risk. The idea of taking off her clothes, of stripping bare without any shield or protection, terrified her. Being naked meant being vulnerable, opening herself up to criticism and horrible comments. In her view, the potential flaw in getting the idea launched might be in finding that brave woman who would willingly sign up to be judged.

Allan shifted in his chair. "Victoria—"

She hated that Preston spread the name confusion to someone else. "Jennifer."

"Does the woman Allan is describing sound like anyone you know?" Preston asked.

She tried not to be flattered since he usually followed a compliment with a subtle slam. "We know a lot of pretty women who take risks."

"That's not what I'm asking you."

But he wasn't asking her. Not really. He was pushing Jennifer aside to highlight Victoria, the woman he viewed as his creation. And it was her fault. She'd nurtured the persona. She opened the door and changed her look and gave her fantasies an outlet. She'd picked a name and set up the life. Blaming him for all of that wasn't fair.

Alan lightly tapped the table. "Are you interested?"

"In stripping in front of a camera so who knows how many people can see?"

"Yes."

"No."

Allan's face fell. "Why?"

"That life doesn't sound like me." It was the woman she wished she could be, but that little girl from Sarnia still had boundaries, lines she feared crossing.

Preston cleared his throat. "It sounds exactly like something Victoria Sinclair would do."

If he had wanted to pick the exact wrong thing to say, he'd done it. "It's too much."

"Fine." His disappointment thumped through the room like a frantic out-of-control heartbeat. "But it's an opportunity to be someone."

"I am someone."

Allan's gaze flipped from Jennifer to Preston and back again. "Don't worry about it."

"Exactly," Preston said. "Some woman will see the opportunity and not be afraid to take it."

"Well, let me leave you two." Allan gathered up his papers and shoved them into a briefcase. He grabbed a card out of the top before shutting it and held it out to her. "Here. If you change your mind, call me. The offer is open."

She watched as Preston showed Allan to the door. She waited until the lock clicked to say anything else. "You think I can't appreciate how this could take off."

But she did. The mix of beauty and sex and news could prove irresistible at the right price. Men paid for less all the time.

"I'm saying, as usual, you go right to the edge and then run away. It's your pattern."

"That's not fair." The observation stung. It wasn't the first time she'd heard the words. Paul had frequently accused her of running when things got tough.

"Isn't it?" Preston reached around her and grabbed a leather binder off the table on his way to the bedroom.

"Where are you going?"

"I know women. I might be able to help Allan find what he needs." Preston flipped through some pages. "Definitely Maryann or Lynne. Both would be perfect."

He named the two most beautiful women in their circle of friends. They were untamed and open. They grabbed life with a gusto that left her envious.

Jennifer had never questioned his fidelity before. He'd never given her a reason, but watching the sly smile inch across his face as he thought about other women made her wonder. All those afternoons while she was at the office or weeks when she was on travel and he was working from home. She'd assumed he kept his days professional. For some reason, the explanation now rang cold.

Two months passed. Allan called three times. He couldn't find the right woman to film the pilot. The Internet was too new and the idea too odd for anyone to jump on board. The longer the days dragged on without a viable candidate, the angrier Preston got at her. He insisted she was wasting the perfect opportunity. He thought her fear made him look bad in front of Allan. As usual, Preston was all about Preston.

But she started thinking about how the idea could impact

her. She'd searched for something her entire life, something that would take her out of Sarnia and eventually out of the politics of an office environment. Her father and sister were artists. Jennifer appreciated a steady paycheck from a big company, but she loved the idea of trying an idea that depended on some piece of her to succeed. She wanted to throw herself into something and try to make it work.

She remembered walking away from Paul in her search for something more. Now that something had dropped right in front of her, and she was terrified to take it. The idea of showing her body, of opening herself up to ridicule, scared the hell out of her. But missing this chance terrified her even more.

Maybe this was wrong. Maybe it was right. Either way, she could help to get it off the ground. There was no reason for an idea to die out of fear. In the end, she jumped and ignored the lack of a safety net.

She leaned back against the kitchen sink and watched Preston pour a glass of wine. "I called Allan. I told him I'd do the pilot. He'll have something for Walt to see and use to hook other investors and media outlets."

Something sparked to life behind Preston's blue eyes. "You'll get naked?"

"Yes."

"What about all those irrational fears of yours?"

She clenched her teeth together and counted to ten. When she opened her mouth again, heat had flooded through her. "They weren't irrational. They were realistic. I don't know any woman who wouldn't change some part of her body."

He cocked his head to the side and stared at her. "What would you change?"

No way was she opening that door. He had rearranged parts of her life already. She refused to let him change anything else. "That's not important. We're talking about the pilot. I'll do it."

He winked at her as his smile grew wide. "I knew you would come around."

The air inside her flattened. He acted like this was a game instead of the biggest decision of her life. "What made you so sure?"

"I know you better than you know yourself."

But he didn't. One man knew her, and he was long gone.

Nineteen

Sometimes having the dream is enough. Most times not.

—Grandma Gladys, *The Duchess*

PAUL DIDN'T HEAR HER COME IN. HE WAS BANGING ON the drums, playing to the song in his head. Sweat dripped off his shoulders and forehead as the beat of the music ran through him.

It wasn't until Wendy stood right in front of him that he even noticed her. He jumped in his seat at the unwanted interruption.

"Hey." He lowered the sticks nice and slow as the flat line of her lips registered in his brain. She was pissed. Any idiot could see that. "I didn't see you come in."

Her fists never left her hips. "You said you'd be home two hours ago."

"I got caught up in this." He was in a friend's studio instead of at his own. He was only four doors down, but it felt like a lifetime away from the place he shared with Brian and Wendy. He paid bills there. Tonight he needed an outlet that didn't house his normal life, so he created here.

"We had dinner plans."

Like he cared about food right now. "Sorry."

"You say that a lot lately."

She had every right to be pissed. He'd come down here to escape from her, from what had become a nightly occurrence—fighting.

Still, despite the attitude and the fact he brought this one on his shoulders, he wasn't in the mood for a scene. The fighting sucked the life out of him. He'd defend and apologize and eventually give in to some degree just to keep peace.

"What do you want from me, Wendy?"

Her eyebrow raised. "A sign you care."

"We live together." To him that meant something. To her it was a first step to something else. He didn't like this need of hers to define the future and cling to that hope instead of living in the moment.

He used to despise Jennifer's ability to separate and remain cold. Now he understood she didn't do it for personal protection. You built the space to keep something for yourself before the headache pounded you to the ground.

She started tapping her foot. "Brian lives there, too."

"So?"

"Clearly being in the house doesn't mean anything more than sharing a place. There's no foundation."

"What are you talking about?"

"It's been years, Paul. I've invested in this relationship. In you."

She brushed her hand over the edge of his drums, and he worried she planned an act of vandalism. She'd never shown the least sign of violence, but her hands shook with what he assumed was pure rage.

"Maybe we should go somewhere else," he suggested.

She looked from him to the drums and back again. "I'm talking about our relationship and you're worried about your damn drums?"

Until she said it, he hadn't even realized he'd made that list of priorities and put her at the bottom. "Sorry." He got up and walked around until he stood in front of her.

"I'd think so."

"Things are going well." He ran a hand up her arm, hoping to comfort her or at least undo some of the damage he'd unknowingly inflicted on her simply by not being ready for dinner on time.

She shrugged out of his hold. "For you."

"I know that's some sort of woman-speak, but I don't get it." His frustration with her, with the situation, with all the pieces of his life he couldn't control, boiled over. "Just tell me what you want from me."

"Commitment." She jabbed him in the middle of the chest.

"You have it."

"Are you really this dense?"

"I gave you that when I agreed you could move in." He winced the second after the words left his mouth. He heard them, saw the shock in her wide eyes, and knew he'd handled the situation all wrong.

"Agreed? Like I forced you to be with me?"

He took a long breath and tried again for calm. "Don't twist my words."

"It's time for you to be an adult, Paul."

The words echoed every complaint Jennifer had ever lodged against him. Looked like no matter how many steps he took forward, he kept leaping backward. The women in his life refused to recognize any progress, and he worried they were right. Hard to imagine half of the world's population being wrong on this one issue.

Wendy threw up her hands. "You are useless."

Like that, the building guilt evaporated. All those struggles with self-worth and bad decisions from being a teen came rushing back at him. "I have a job and a few hobbies. I make some money off my music and pay all my bills."

"I know all that."

"Then tell me where I'm failing you."

She held up her hand with the back to him. "Here."

The anger whooshed back out of him. He got the message. She wanted a damn ring.

He wasn't ready to give her one. "Wendy, we've talked about this."

"No, I've talked about it and you've ignored me or talked around it. You never take a stand or give me an answer."

Guilty. He couldn't deny any of it. "I like things how they are now."

"The problem is clear." She didn't wait for him to ask. "I'm not Jennifer."

Everything inside him crumbled. Hearing Jennifer's name on Wendy's lips was too much. "Don't do that."

"You are pining for a woman who dumped you years ago. Do you think she even still remembers you?"

He blocked the verbal blows and concentrated on staying on his feet and in the conversation. "This has nothing to do with Jennifer. It's about us."

She flipped her hand around and showed him the palm. "Save it."

He would never understand women. "You're the one who wanted to talk."

"I'm going to dinner." Wendy picked up the jacket Paul hadn't even seen her drape over the back of the chair.

He exhaled. While he appreciated the relatively quick end to the fight, he was sick of all the arguing. "Give me a second to wash up."

"Forget it."

"What?"

"Brian is taking me."

Her comments didn't make any sense. "I'm not invited to dinner with you?"

"Not tonight. Not until you figure out who and what you want." She turned and stormed toward the door. Not walking and not even running. This was a stomping, with a head-down plow to get away from him.

"Wendy—"

She didn't bother to turn around. "I mean it, Paul."

The door slammed behind her and then . . . nothing. The lonely seconds ticked by. He sat in silence for a full five minutes before he grabbed the phone.

Neil picked up on the first ring, but Paul didn't give him time to say anything. "It's time."

"What?"

Paul heard the confusion in his friend's voice. "To say how you told me so."

"Wendy?"

"Yeah."

Neil swore. "The marriage thing? Man, I'm sorry." And he sounded it. Being the good friend he was, there was no gloating or the promised *I told you so*. "Is it over?"

"No, but I think she's given me an ultimatum."

"Did she say that? Give you a deadline?"

"Not in so many words."

Neil blew out a breath. "I'll be there in a few minutes."

Jennifer liked Walt from the first minute she met him. Naked News was his idea. He could have been a jerk and a pervert or a mixture of the two. Instead, he was a forty-something business-man with thinning brown hair, a wedding ring, and a smile that made her comfortable.

He sat across from her at a metal conference table in a single-room office on the bottom floor of an older building in down-town Toronto. Nothing fancy or showy. This was a place where real work happened without the benefit of office staff or expensive furnishings.

At one end of the room was a wall draped with fabric and a small screen suspended nearby. A camera stood in front of the filming area while a man fiddled with the lens. They agreed to do a test run here and then try the pilot in a rented studio only if she was comfortable going forward with the plan.

With Preston at her side, as he insisted he be when he declared himself her agent, Walt spelled out what he expected of the pilot. Most impressive, his gaze never dipped below her chin. He kept it professional, which in turn eased some of the anxiety jumping around inside her.

Despite everything, she was at heart pretty shy. She didn't grow up in a house that welcomed nudity. Her parents weren't conven-tional and neither was her upbringing, but sexuality wasn't dis-cussed in the open either. She'd learned what she'd learned from Heather and the Duchess, who believed all young women should be armed with the fundamentals.

Stripping her clothes off in front of men she didn't know would be a huge step from the past she clung to. Letting someone tape it and then show it to other women and possible investors was well out of Jennifer's normal range.

Preston loved it. He showed her off as if he'd invented her. In a way, maybe he had. She walked into the studio with her best Victoria swagger. She wore a sexy wrap navy dress and her hair long and straight. She answered only to Victoria Sinclair and carried the self-confidence that came with the name and not with her own.

"I know this is a bit uncomfortable," Walt said as he twirled the pen around in his fingers.

Preston touched his hand against hers. Didn't hold it. More like patted it. "She's fine."

This one time she didn't want Preston speaking for her. "It's okay, Walt. Really."

"I don't expect the test to be perfect on the first shot. You'll have some nerves. We'll work through them and get you comfortable and keep editing until we get a run we all like."

She appreciated Walt's words. Loved the fact he talked to her and not through Preston. "Thank you."

Walt's smile was warm and respectful. "I want this to work, and the only way that happens is if you can sell it."

"She can." Preston leaned against her, moving his body into Walt's line of vision while speaking.

She bit the inside of her cheek to keep from screaming at Preston and telling him to shut up. "I can."

"Well, I don't doubt that." Walt poured a cup of coffee and slid it in her direction. "We'll relax for a few minutes and then take some shots for lighting."

Preston stood up. "Delaying is only going to make it worse. We should start."

"We go when she's ready." Walt snapped the comment at Preston before turning back to her. "It's just news, weather, and sports. You read it every day. This time you'll do it out loud."

She glanced down at the paper in front of her but only saw a black blur of lines. Her insides were shaking too hard for her to concentrate. "I practiced the lines."

"Good." Walt glanced at the cameraman behind them and shook his head. "Whenever you're ready."

She spoke before Preston could answer for her. "I'm ready."

She doubted she could even stand up. The bones in her knees had melted into liquid. But time was money, and she was not about to let her worries cost these men more than was necessary.

Before she could run or come to her senses, she stood up and walked to the screen set up on the other side of the small room. Standing there in front of three men, one who had seen her naked every day for years and two others who didn't know much more about her than her name, was a surreal experience. She expected a priest to jump out at any second and scold her just for being there.

In front of the screen, with the lights blazing and the soft murmur of male voices shadowed in front of her, she struggled with an attack of jumping nerves. The first two times she tried to speak, she stumbled.

She'd known her name when she stepped up here, but it was beyond her right now. And she still had all of her clothes on.

While Walt said a steady stream of encouraging words, Preston stood with his arms folded across his chest. One look at his face and she knew she was blowing it.

The answer for overcoming the anxiety was easy. She needed to pretend he wasn't there. That she was talking directly to a guy on his couch, a guy who liked pretty women and wanted to know the football scores.

She inhaled nice and deep, then nodded to the cameraman. "I'm ready."

Walt stepped out from behind the equipment. "We can do a few more practice lines before we turn the camera on."

"I'm okay."

"It's no problem. I don't mind."

The reassuring tone to Walt's voice unknotted her tangled nerves. She saw his face and heard the buzz of the lights. She knew they were waiting on her and would continue to do so, but letting the minutes tick by would only prolong the initial agony. She had to try it and see.

If she hated it, she would walk out. That was the deal she had with Walt. Having an "out" gave her the confidence she needed to start.

She rolled her shoulders back and looked straight into the camera. She could do this. Own it and conquer it.

She smiled, letting the last of her nervousness fuel her resolve. "Let's get started."

The light on the camera flashed to red just as she shifted her head and let her dark hair cascade down her back. Her fingers moved to the belt holding her dress together. "I'm Victoria Sinclair, and this is Naked News."

Twenty

Beautiful naked women and information—
it's the perfect combination.

—Victoria Sinclair

"I WANT YOU TO DO IT." WALT DELIVERED HIS STATEMENT over lunch a month later.

The water sloshed over the side of Jennifer's water glass as she rushed to return it to the table. "Me?"

"You are a natural in front of the camera. It responds to you."

She should have known he was talking about the professional angle. That's who he was. Even without Preston there, Walt's character didn't waver.

And the compliments made her smile.

Preston barely acknowledged her some days. He'd be furious when he found out she stepped out with Walt and didn't issue an invitation. In Preston's mind, he made her decisions. In her head, he was nothing more than a boyfriend, and even that was a question lately.

Preston could throw out a line and think it made all the bad stuff before it go away. As if she was so shallow and needy as to be satisfied with kernels of affection rather than true affection.

With Walt, the words carried a note of genuine appreciation. She knew his compliments came from an honest place with him. He was a salesman of sorts and a successful businessman first, but he could deliver a line and make her believe it.

She toyed with how much she should admit and decided to honor him with the truth. "I was surprised."

"About?"

"How much I enjoyed the taping."

"I could tell." He sat back in his chair as the waiter cleared the plates and left. "You nailed it in two takes."

Pride spilled through her. She'd always known she was smart and sort of pretty in a small-town, nonthreatening way. But in front of the camera, she felt special.

She didn't worry about the thickness of her thighs or the size of her breasts. Her body came alive, every nerve ending tingling as she talked and let the clothing fall with each word.

It was about being in charge. For so long, Preston had tried to call every shot in her life. Sure, she owed this opportunity to him, but this was something that belonged solely to her. He couldn't manage or direct it. He couldn't step in and do it for her. It was all about her up there.

"The plan was for me to do the pilot to lure other women into participating." She repeated the deal to avoid any miscommunication.

"Plans change."

"It's a huge step." She unfolded and refolded her napkin. "I mean, I work in an office. I run meetings and get people where they need to be."

"And I'm sure you're good at it."

She wound one end of the cloth napkin around her finger until the tip turned white. "I don't even use the same name there as I do with you."

"You could always think of Victoria as your stage name."

"That's how I view it." That's exactly what it was. A name that covered certain aspects of her, but not all of her. Preston missed the fundamental distinction and merged the personalities until Jennifer ceased to exist.

"Nothing more than a pseudonym for your protection and privacy."

Heather had raised that issue several times, and Jennifer ignored it. "Protection?"

"I can't promise every one who watches you will be decent or even nice. There are jerks and scumbags out there, but you could run into them just as easy in a big office."

"And I have."

Walt tapped his fingers on the table. "May I make an honest observation?"

"Of course."

"You want to do this. I can see it in your face. You talk about the project and your eyes get big and your breathing kicks up. I don't see the same enthusiasm for your other job."

It was as if he could see right through her. She'd grown weary and bored in an office environment. The challenge was gone.

But that didn't make this the right step. "Change is scary."

"That's why it's called change instead of fun."

She laughed.

"Look," Walt leaned in. "The choice is yours. I can tell Preston to keep looking for another woman, or you can take it over and make it your own. The choice is totally yours. You won't get any pressure from me."

"I appreciate that."

"I don't pretend to know everything. I just think you should headline the broadcast. You're the one. I can feel it."

That made two of them. "What makes you so sure?"

"I've built a reputation and earned a lot of money spotting talent and nurturing it. There is this undefinable quality some people have." He pointed at her. "You possess it. It spills out of you."

The words piled around her like a protective shield against all of her fears. "I wish I was as sure as you were."

"Think about it this way. If we find someone else tomorrow, how are you going to feel to hand over the reins and let someone else run with it?"

Anger simmered inside her at the thought. "Furious."

"Then I think you might have your answer."

Between the time it took for her to listen and to blink, her answer crystallized in her mind. "So what exactly is the plan from here?"

That fast, Walt morphed into businessman mode. He dragged a notebook out of his jacket pocket and flipped through a few pages until he found something and started reading. "You'll be the audio and visual component of a comedy newsletter called *The Daily Dirt*. From there, we build interest and expand to short add-on segments on other programs."

It was what he didn't say that had her stomach flopping. "You have more in mind. I can feel it."

He shrugged. "Eventually, I'd like Naked News to be a self-sustaining program. Not an add-on or short segment. A full broadcast with loyal paying viewers and numerous anchors. With you taking the lead, of course. With success, I doubt finding other women will be a problem."

She'd be in charge. She'd have a boss but be the first and temporarily only anchor. That amounted to a lot of control. Walt had
indicated he would listen to her suggestions, and she didn't doubt
that promise. She'd also make sure it was a provision in any contract they entered into.

"Interesting." That's all she said, but it took all the energy she
had to keep her butt in the chair. Bouncing around and squealing
with excitement wasn't all that professional, and she wanted to
show him she could be the face of Naked News and he wouldn't
lose his fortune.

"We'll get started, and you'll be the queen."

The idea was so foreign to her. "I've never been the object of
that much male attention before."

He laughed.

The rough sound confused her. "What?"

"I'm betting you have."

Flattery was a wonderful thing. She liked him. Trusted him.
And boy, did she want this. Like, every-part-of-her-trembled-
and-shook wanted this.

She reached her hand across the table. "Sounds like we have a
deal."

Three months later, she sat at her make-up chair in the make-
shift Naked News office and scanned the printouts Walt had just
handed her. Line after line, and they all said the same thing: the
risk had panned out.

She had an hour before they taped. Hair and make-up would
start soon. For the first month, she did all of those things herself.
Now she had someone come in and help her. She also had two
other anchors recently join her on camera. She'd trained them and
welcomed the company.

Being up there alone in front of a room of cameraman and a producer could be daunting. Having someone else on the stage made it more of a sisterhood moment. Being one of the group also meant she could concentrate on the part of the broadcast she enjoyed the most—the news.

"Have you seen this?" She glanced up at Preston, who was always hovering nearby.

"What is it"

"The newest numbers." She almost screamed the news. It bubbled up inside her, begging to get out. "We're up to ten thousand subscribers. It's only been three months."

"I couldn't be more pleased," Walt said.

They'd exceeded all expectations. She'd left her daytime job to focus on Naked News. That gamble turned out to be a wise and potentially lucrative business move on her part.

And it was just the beginning. "I think we need more."

Preston hadn't stopped looking through the papers or even bothered to look up. Walt was paying full attention to her. "Of?"

"The show."

For once, Preston didn't take over the conversation or tell her how wrong she was in her line of thinking. He stood there, staring down at her and actually listened as she talked with Walt. "You should buy out the contract and convince the other investors and the show's producers to make Naked News its own program instead of an add-on to something else."

Preston pressed one hand against the back of her chair and watched her through the mirror. His expression stayed blank, but his body language was open, as if he were listening for a change.

"That's always been the long-term plan," Walt said.

"I get that, but there's no need to wait."

Walt leaned against the table in front of her, giving her his full focus. "The longer it goes on, the higher the viewership will be and the easier to land a full show. It's a matter of positioning for the best possible price."

"I get that, but you could strike now while you have total control and before the bureaucracy rushes in. The investors become the board of directors and we move."

Walt smiled. "Makes sense."

"There's enough material." The words rushed through her, and she had to swallow a few times to get them out.

"Have you thought about the downside?" Preston asked.

She couldn't think of a single negative. "Which is?"

"You might end up with a smaller role on the show."

All her excitement vanished. He'd always had the power to do that to her. The wrong word at the wrong time and she felt as if she'd been kicked in the stomach.

"What do you mean?" she asked.

"More time likely means more anchors. You're already down to news only."

Walt waved off Preston's concerns. "Absolutely not. She asked for the news segment and I gave it to her. She is my lead."

Preston shifted until he stood half in front of her, blocking her view of Walt. "I think you should wait."

"Why?"

"It's prudent."

Preston was wrong on this. She could feel it. Following his gut was the wrong choice. "I'm only suggesting this because I think it is best for *my* show."

Because this wasn't about him. Not anymore. She's the one who took the risk. She's the one who stood up there every night and opened her body up to being picked apart and dissected by the most vicious of critics.

If she was honest, that fear of being ripped apart had never materialized. The men who watched the show were fans and very supportive. She received all sorts of letters praising her, and very few that fell in the scary pile.

No one talked about the flaws she saw every time she looked in the mirror. No one called her names or made assumptions about who she was based on her decision to take off her clothes. Her immediate family knew, and her father struggled a bit with the idea of some of his friends watching his daughter, but he stayed positive.

But still the pressure of looking as good as possible and the never-ending panic of having someone judge her as wanting never went away. All those insecurities, ingrained in high school and nurtured by life since then, silently smacked her around from time to time.

Her friend Andrea and sister Heather thought she was brave. That was the greatest compliment of all. That other women could look at what she was doing and appreciate the value of it. Jennifer just wished she saw more of Heather and Andrea these days.

Between the work and Preston's demands for attention, Jennifer had very little time for her friends. She felt more isolated even though she had never been more exposed.

Worse, she'd lost all contact with Paul. The years had ticked by without one of those unexpected phone calls or chance meetings. Sometimes, when she was alone and allowed her mind to wander, she dreamed about him. He was her first love and, she feared, her only true one.

"I'll consider it." Walt's voice broke through the silence. "Your argument is well reasoned and smart."

She snapped back to the present and saw the deep frown on Preston's face when Walt picked her view over his. "Good."

"Now, it's time to get to work." Walt gave her a thumbs-up then left.

Preston watched him go. "That was a mistake."

"Maybe."

"You'll regret it."

"If I do, I'll have no one to blame but myself." And for some reason that felt good.

Twenty-One

When one opportunity ends, another begins.
—Grandma Gladys, The Duchess

THE DAY HAD BEEN CRAP. A BIG, HEAPING PILE OF CRAP.

Paul slammed the car door and wrapped his hand around his aching wrist. Last time he'd try to catch a coworker as he fell off a ladder.

He wanted to rub his eyes, but they burned from too little sleep and too many hours on the job. He should have stopped for drops, but he'd just wanted to get home to a shower and his bed. As soon as his head hit the pillow he knew he'd sleep for a week. Maybe longer.

This project had been hell. It took him away from home for more than five weeks, installing pipes and otherwise engaging in back-breaking labor for days on end. He relished working outside, but his muscles screamed for rest.

The drums could wait.

Hell, Wendy could wait.

Shower, sandwich, pillow. That was the only order that mattered. If Wendy tried to talk him to death, he'd pretend to fall asleep, though heaven knew he wouldn't have to fake that.

He fumbled with his keys at the front door. His breath hissed out of him when he twisted his hand the wrong way and aggravated his injury. "Damn."

He finally shoved the front door open and was surprised to see the studio dark. The usual nightlight near the kitchen counter was even off.

The timing didn't make sense. It was only seven, hardly past dinner time. Probably meant Wendy and Brian went out. He couldn't blame them since he wasn't supposed to be home until tomorrow.

That was the only good thing about the injury. He got to escape a bit early, but not until after he'd spent hours waiting for a medical release. The paperwork and inevitable questioning about workplace safety would be unbearable next week, but he couldn't dwell on that now. It wasn't in his evening plans.

He dumped his bag on the hardwood floor and stalked through the darkness, past the stairway to the loft and into the kitchen. He opened the fridge, even thought about downing a beer, but the shower called. He wouldn't feel human until he'd washed the grime off.

Each bedroom had a bathroom. Brian's was upstairs. Paul's was in the bedroom off the family room. He headed there.

He didn't hear the rustling until he was on top of the door. He didn't have to reach for the phone or call the police. The lights were off in there as well, but he didn't mistake the noise. Shuffling and panting. Low murmurs and the whisper of Wendy's voice.

She had a man in there.

His heart stopped. Actually stammered to a stop and brought him to a standstill with his hand frozen just inches from pushing the door fully open.

Through the crack, he could see bare legs and the movement of sheets over the mattress. A groan. Begging.

He forced his hand to move and shoved the door open until it bounced against the wall behind it. At the crashing sound, the figures on the bed jumped apart.

Paul saw a blur of skin and blue sheets. When his mind focused again, he watched Wendy curl up near the headboard with material clenched in her fist and her eyes wide with horror.

"Paul . . ." She shook her head as if trying to make his image disappear.

His gaze moved to the other person crowded against the pillows. Dark hair and a slight build.

"Man, I can explain," Brian said.

Paul tried to open his mouth. Tried to make sense of the scene in front of him as his mind replayed every moment and every conversation of the last year. The pieces fell together. His roommate and his girlfriend eating dinner and watching movies. They shifted to a couple and never bothered to fill him in.

Wendy scrambled to her knees. "It's not what you think."

Paul found his voice. "What the hell are you talking about?"

"It's . . ." Wendy looked to Brian and then back to Paul, but no words came out.

They didn't have to. He had eyes. He could see them, close his eyes and hear them. The memory was burned in his brain.

"You're sleeping with Brian." Paul gagged on the words as he choked back the bile rushing up his throat.

She scampered toward him, dragging the sheet behind her and exposing Brian's chest. "Paul, please listen to me."

"No." The word came out as a harsh whisper. Paul didn't even recognize the sound as his own.

Tears ran down her cheeks. "I didn't mean for this to happen."

"You used our bed." That fact pricked him the most. They could have granted him some dignity and used Brian's room, but no.

The sharpness of the betrayal stabbed at every visible inch of skin. They didn't just cheat. They ripped everything to shreds and made it impossible for his mind to function without revulsion spilling through him.

He trusted them. Shared his concerns with Brian and his life with Wendy. While he thought he was getting support, he was really pushing her to someone else. Someone who lived right there and pretended loyalty.

Paul grabbed the door frame as a wave of dizziness threatened to take him down. Brian shifted as if to get out of bed, but Paul stopped him with a deadly glare. "Don't."

Brian sat back down hard. "We should go into the other room and talk about it."

Geography wasn't going to make this better or wipe the visions of their naked bodies from his head. Paul could barely breathe. "Why?"

Wendy slipped off the mattress and stood in front of Paul. "How can you ask that? We have to work this through."

That she could think she'd ever mean anything to him again stunned him. "There's nothing to figure out."

Her wet eyes pleaded with him. "We can work through this."

He stood there, letting the sudden quiet wash through him. For the first time in a very long while, he didn't know what to do. Hit Brian or run. Shake her or unload on what he thought of her. He wanted to swear and curse.

"I'll be out by the weekend." Paul didn't know where the words came from, but they were the right ones.

Wendy took the final step, closing the remaining distance between them. "No!"

Brian stood beside her. "Paul, don't do this, man."

He looked from one to the other, to the two people he should be able to trust more than anyone else, and he felt nothing but a cold calm. No heat or passion. No pain or anger.

Those would come later. Rage brewed right under the surface. He felt it heating up and planned to wallow in it when he was alone, but not now. He refused to give them the satisfaction.

They'd hollowed him out and left nothing behind. He didn't know a body could hurt like this.

"It just happened." Wendy's gaze skidded away from his face as she said it.

His brain jump-started. Suddenly he had to know how long they been screwing behind his back. "How many times?"

"What?" She stammered out the question.

"It's simple. How often? How many days . . . or is it more like months?" Paul wanted the details if only as a way to strengthen his mind against her and guarantee something like this would never happen again.

Brian winced. "It's not—"

Damn. "A long time then."

The anger came at Paul in a rush. He'd been so damn blind. He'd spent hours wallowing in guilt over Wendy and his inability to meet her relationship demands. And she'd been laughing at him while she screwed his friend.

The betrayal threatened to knock him over. The exhaustion faded away, leaving behind a trail of throbbing pain mixed with an almost homicidal need to hurt her.

He had to get out of there.

"Be gone tomorrow, and I'll come back to get my things." He turned to leave, not having any idea where to go.

Wendy wrapped her fingers around his arm and turned him back to face her. "Listen to me."

He glanced at her hand and wondered why he couldn't even feel her touch. "Let go."

Something in his voice must have reached her because her hand dropped and the tears fell faster. He saw it and didn't care. He wanted to hurt her, to shred her insides like she was doing to him.

"Tomorrow. Gone." He couldn't say anything else.

He walked and kept walking until he hit his car. He didn't remember picking up his duffel bag or putting the keys in the ignition. The next time his brain focused, he was sitting in Neil's driveway. That he didn't crash or injure anyone was nothing short of a miracle.

He had no idea how long he sat there in the cold car as the darkness enveloped him. When he woke up, he was in Neil's guestroom.

Twenty-Two

Know your limits.

—Grandma Gladys, The Duchess

JENNIFER SAW HIM ACROSS THE CROWDED BAR AND her heart rate spiked. After all this time and how much her life had changed, he still owned her heart.

The randomness of them being together now in the same place, on the same night, struck her. Preston had an unexpected meeting next door. He dropped her off here to wait while he worked. Or supposedly worked. She no longer understood what he did with his time, and his violent mood swings made questioning him too risky.

She tried to blend in. As months turned to nearly two years at Naked News, she became noticed more often, though still not as much as she thought would happen. But going out and just being Jennifer grew tougher as the subscriptions rose.

Tonight, she stood with her head balanced against a wooden post and stared at her past. For all the people who knew her as Victoria, Paul was the one who loved her as Jennifer. He'd never said the words. Didn't have to. They hovered between them, unsaid but vibrating with life.

In the quiet of her mind, she watched him. He was as handsome as she remembered. All guy and tough on the outside but sweet underneath. Blondish-brown hair fell over his forehead, just begging for fingers to run through it.

She couldn't hear his laugh, but she remembered the rich sound. His shoulders shook and his eyes lit up as he nodded at something Neil said. They chatted up the bartender and snuck peeks at the game on the television behind him. Their bond appeared as strong as ever, which filled her with a humble satisfaction.

Paul deserved good friends and good times. He deserved so much.

From her vantage point behind a post and through crowds of people, she could see the blonde two seats down throw I'm-available looks in Paul's direction. So far, he wasn't catching the hint. Didn't even seem to notice.

Jennifer smiled at his lack of ego. He never did understand his appeal. He failed to notice when Tracie flirted with him. His laser-like focus kept him moving forward.

Not that he'd been celibate. Hardly that. Jennifer heard rumors now and then. Knew he'd lived with a woman named Wendy but hadn't heard much about her recently. Jennifer stood up on her tiptoes looking for a wedding band, but she was too far away to get a good peek.

Every now and then Heather would hear something, or people in Jennifer's social circle would mention seeing Paul. They didn't run with the same people, but they went in and out of the same neighborhoods, so their friends would talk.

More than once she'd asked someone to pass a message to Paul that "Jennifer said hi" but she never heard back. Figured on some level that was best.

Still, she was amazed she didn't see him more often. She'd sure been tempted to seek him out and watch him play with his band from the safe distance at the back of the room. Working up the nerve had been the issue.

So was explaining her absence to Preston. He didn't even like her hanging out with Heather. And he knew all about Paul. Not the details, but bits and pieces. Likely enough to ferret out her true feelings.

"You ready to go?" As if she'd conjured him up, Preston stepped in front of her, blocking her view of Paul.

Preston's eyes were glassy and wild. He kept glancing around and shifting. A mass of constant motion, which was a new thing he'd picked up.

She focused on this thin lips. "Are you okay?"

"Yeah, why?"

"You seem . . . funny."

His usual detached demeanor had been replaced with twitching. "We need to head out."

Leaving would be a relief. "Okay."

Still not sure what was happening or the reason behind Preston's jumpy behavior, she put her arm through Preston's. For the briefest of moments she let her gaze touch on Paul. A visual caress for a second in that one last look.

Something on her face had Preston spinning around. He followed her stare.

"What are you . . ." His eyebrows lifted. "Ah, I get it."

Her blood froze. "What?"

"Now I see what has you so excited. Paul's here. Perfect." Preston didn't run his hands together like a scene is some bad movie, but he looked like he could.

"For what?"

He smiled with a coldness that chilled her. "I'm fine with it. He's a friend. You're close."

Every cell in her body whirled in panic. The thought of her worlds colliding here, like this, with Preston on edge and Paul relaxed, made the room spin around her. "What are you talking about?"

"Did you say hello to him? Catch up on old times?"

"No."

"Now, that's no way to treat an old lover."

"Preston, don't—"

"Let's go relive old times, shall we?" Preston turned toward the bar.

She grabbed his arm and tugged until he faced her again. It took all of her strength and will to stop his tracks. "I want to leave."

"We can talk, maybe exchange some stories about you. We're all grown-ups."

She wasn't convinced that was true at the moment. "We're supposed to meet the others in an hour."

She didn't want to go out or haunt the clubs. Everything inside her screamed to rush home and hide there. This was her nightmare. She's dreamed about seeing Paul again, but not like this.

Preston's smirk morphed into a frown. "Why are you so nervous?"

Terrified was more like it. "I'm not."

"I was thinking we should get together with him. You know I've been wanting us to make some new friends and try a few adventures."

She knew what he really meant, and it had nothing to do with friendship. This was part of Preston's pushing of her boundaries. He wanted to take her to dark, forbidden places she didn't want to go.

"No, Preston."

He stood there for a second before a smile broke over his face. "You win this round."

She never won. Not with him. She might not be strong enough to leave him, but she was smart enough to get that.

"I think we should get out of here."

"And I believe in giving a woman what she wants."

She didn't question her luck in him dropping the subject. Instead, she moved him out the door as fast as possible.

"You're Paul, right?"

Dark hair and an expensive suit. Paul knew exactly who this guy was. He'd seen him around. Heard stories. The guy was some business genius.

Preston, the man Jennifer lived with, probably loved.

He'd been sitting at the table in the bar, staring for the last twenty minutes. He'd been in the same place last week, but Paul had only caught a glimpse of him that night. Something had twitched at the back of his neck, and when he turned, he'd seen Preston shuffling toward the door.

Paul got the hint. Clearly, the man wanted attention. Paul wasn't in the mood for a fight and certainly didn't want to think about Jennifer. He didn't want to think of any woman, really. The situation with Wendy had rubbed him raw.

She called every day and he ignored her. They were over and he was looking forward to some time alone. No more jumping from relationship to relationship. A guy could only take so much crazy in his life.

He would have left the bar now, shoved this smirking jerk to the side and hit the door, except that he was meeting Neil and a few other friends. So Paul sat there and shook hands with the guy who now had the right to touch Jennifer every night.

The thought kicked him as hard as Wendy's betrayal. If he were being honest, even harder.

"I have something for you." The guy's voice was as smooth as scotch.

Paul hated the other man on sight. "What?"

"Here." Preston slid a piece of paper across the bar in Paul's direction.

It was all a bit too spy-like for Paul's taste. If the guy had something to say, he should just say it. Playing games was not his thing. Engaging in some sort of showdown with this jackass didn't sit well either.

Paul knew he no longer had the right to fight for Jennifer. That was this guy's role now.

"What is it?" he asked without turning the paper over to read it. If the guy wanted to play games, fine, but Paul wasn't participating.

Preston hesitated, his gaze narrowing. "Jennifer's private cell number."

Paul cringed at the way the guy said her name, all possessive and demanding, like he owned her or something. But there was something else. A desperation that pulsed just under the surface.

One thought lead to another until Paul's mind went barreling in a dozen directions, most of them bad. "Is she okay? Did something happen?"

Despite his women-free vow, he'd break it for her. If she needed him, he'd figure out a way to be there for her. To hell with self-preservation.

"She wants to talk to you."

"About what?"

"You should ask her."

The conversation bordered on crazy. Jennifer's boyfriend throwing them together. What kind of guy did that?

"Tell me what's going on," Paul said.

"That's between the two of you."

But there was nothing between them. Hadn't been for years. And there was no way this guy wanted to take them all back there. Paul wasn't even sure he could go if invited. Every time Jennifer left him, she took a piece of his heart with her. He didn't have much left to spare.

He shook his head. "I don't understand."

"Hey." Neil slid onto the barstool next to Paul. "What's up?"

"What you do from here is your choice." Preston walked away without another word.

"Who was that?" Neil reached for the bowl of peanuts and slid them to him.

"Preston."

Neil's mouth dropped open. "Jennifer's Preston?"

The words shot through Paul and landed right in the center of his chest like a dead weight. "Yeah."

"Did I miss a fight or something?"

"He wants to me to call Jennifer." Paul turned the scrap of white paper over in his hands. He stared at the numbers and memorized them without trying.

"For God's sake, why?"

"No idea."

"Are you going to?"

He balled up the paper in his fist. "Hell, no."

But he knew he would.

Paul picked up the receiver and slammed it back down again. He'd purposely left his cell in the car to cut down on the temptation to call her.

It had been less than twenty-four hours since Preston handed him Jennifer's number, and he'd thought about nothing but placing that call. Weakness ate at his gut every minute. Neil had offered to take the paper and get rid of it, but it was too late. The numbers flashed in Paul's mind whether he was awake or asleep.

Some great cosmic joke kept throwing him right into Jennifer's path. It had been years, but hearing her name brought it all back. The soft feel of her skin and sexy goodness of her laugh. The body. The face. That incredible mind.

It was so tempting to see what she wanted, if she wanted something, and hear her voice.

But this felt wrong. Jennifer didn't contact him. He hadn't heard anything about her having trouble, though he went out of his way not to hear things about her. If something bad had happened, Heather would have called. That was the unspoken promise when they saw each other the last time.

Then there was the look on the jerk's face as he handed over the number. Smug and self-satisfied. Paul tried to imagine what someone like Jennifer would see in that guy. Money and power were seductive beasts, but he'd never thought Jennifer would get sucked into all that shallow crap.

He stared at the phone one more time.

He should get up. Go out and get a beer. Call Neil and catch a game. Anything but pick up that phone and punch in the numbers.

The receiver was in his hand before he finished the thought. With each ring, he prayed she wasn't around. If her voicemail picked up, he had no idea what he would say.

He'd hang up. Yeah, that was the plan. She had this one chance before he banished the number from his brain.

The phone rang a third time. One more and he was free.

Jennifer stood in the middle of her closet and raced to pull her turtleneck over her head. Her head poked through the second before she performed a perfect diving grab for the phone.

She hit the button on the fourth ring. "Hello?"

Only dead air greeted her. She started to disconnect before she heard it. The slight puff of breathing.

This was her private line. She didn't get crank calls here because so few people had access to the number.

"Hello?" She put enough anger in her voice to let the person on the other end know she wasn't in the mood for games.

"Jennifer."

The husky whisper made her eyes close. An unexpected wave of happiness swept through her. Being connected to him even through this tenuous feed provided a lifeline she didn't even know she needed.

"Paul." She wanted to say more, to be witty and ask all the right questions, but the one word was enough.

He must have seen her the other night at the bar or talked to Heather. The possibilities ran through Jennifer's mind until the nosiness threatened to overtake her.

"How did you get this number?" She used all of her energy to keep her voice neutral. She had nothing left to fuel her muscles and keep her on her feet.

She slid down to the comforter, hunching over the phone as she pressed it tight against her skin. Anything to be closer to him. Anything to hear the warm caress of his voice in her ear.

"Preston gave it to me."

A cold wash of reality poured over her. Preston, the one name she never uttered or even thought about in comparison to Paul. Preston was trying to taint her feelings and erase her past.

He wanted to drag her memories into his lifestyle and ruin the good thoughts she still had for Paul. She refused to let that happen.

"Jennifer?" The scratchy edge to Paul's voice didn't leave when he cleared his throat. "Are you okay?"

Her shoulders slumped from the weight of everything crashing in on her. She dropped her forehead to her hand and massaged her temples.

"Yes." The word sounded false in her ears. She knew Paul would see through the lie.

"Why did Preston tell me to call you?" Confusion filled Paul's rough voice.

"I don't know." But she did.

Preston knew Paul was her greatest weakness. Preston wanted to bring someone else into their relationship, and she'd resisted. She didn't want any part of that life.

Handing Paul to her as an option was a brilliant move. The temptation to see him, touch him, was so great that she almost gave in. Would if Paul gave even the slightest indication he missed her.

"Jennifer, I—"

Instead of spelling it out, she went for the abbreviated version. The details weren't necessary. "Preston likes to play games."

Paul let out a deep breath. When he spoke again, his words shook. "I can't do this."

She wiped the tears from her eyes. "I know."

"Seeing you would . . ."

"I know." She did.

Paul wasn't in a good place, wasn't strong enough to turn her down. She could hear it in every word he spoke. Felt it as if it traveled through the phone.

He was pure temptation. She needed him so badly, so desperately. Part of her wanted to ignore his pleas and explore whatever they could have together. But the bigger, smarter part of her knew being together like this would destroy everything.

He was clean and good. Not perfect, but their time had been precious. She refused to stain that with Preston's twisted fantasies.

"I don't think we should meet. It's not like last time," Paul said.

She nodded her head, unable to speak as she choked back tears.

"The timing is—"

"Wrong," she croaked out. "Yeah, I know."

She sat and held the phone, listening to his steady breathing and enjoying the silence, knowing it was all they should have.

After a few minutes, he broke the quiet. "Promise me something."

"Anything." In that moment she would have knit him the moon if she could.

"Stay strong." Then he hung up the phone.

Twenty-Three

Success doesn't mean everything.

—Grandma Gladys, The Duchess

JENNIFER HAD ALWAYS PRIDED HERSELF ON BEING ABLE to read people. She believed in Zodiac signs and had started investigating tarot cards. She understood there was something more in the world than the tangible things she could feel and see.

None of that explained what was happening to her. Naked News had made her famous in many circles. Her appearance on *Howard Stern* the year before took the show from subscribers in the tens of thousands to more than a quarter of a million. Now they had more than six million hits per month.

She'd had numerous television appearances and interviews. *Entertainment Tonight* had her on repeatedly. She no longer worried about being in front of people or what people would say. She'd ventured so far beyond that.

When needed, she stripped off Jennifer from Sarnia and tucked her away for private. She put on her Victoria Sinclair personality cloak and wowed them far beyond Canada.

Money and opportunities constantly came her way. The directors at Naked News listened to her views. She trained all of the new anchors. In many ways, she'd gone from a mere employee to someone who helped run the show. She had a cut of the franchise and the fat bank account to prove it.

She quietly thanked the owners every day for taking her seriously and including her. They never made her feel little or unimportant. Every promise Walt had made had been fulfilled.

Her professional life was on fire.

Her personal life was exploding into a million terrified and lonely pieces.

Preston made every minute miserable. She'd long ago gone from liking him to tolerating him. She didn't want him guiding her. Didn't even want to see him most days. He'd gone from controlling her wardrobe to picking at everything she did and said. He acted like she didn't have a brain and wasn't worthy of his time.

But the slow destruction of her mental hold on reality was the worst. They'd have arguments, and he'd later deny they even spoke. He started leaving the apartment in the morning and not coming back until late and reeking of cheap perfume.

Today was one step too far. She stared down at her bank statement and tried to make sense of all the withdrawals.

"What are you doing?" His voice slithered through the apartment as he headed for the door, adjusting his tie.

"Did you use my bank card?" She turned around to face him with the paper still clenched in her fist.

He stared her up and down, judging but not seeing her. The dismissal showed in every muscle. "I have my own."

A typical nonanswer. That's all he gave lately. He didn't even try to explain or excuse his behavior. He just acted like everything he did was right and everything she thought was wrong.

"I have all of these deductions listed, and I didn't do any of them."

His eyes narrowed. "You kept taking out money. Don't you remember?"

The room danced in front of her eyes, but she adjusted her stance. She would not back down on this one. No matter how angry or belittling he became. "When?"

"Last week."

Everything shifted and kept moving. It was as if her brain had deteriorated overnight. She'd spent hours dissecting their conversations and rerunning his denials until she thought she was going insane.

"What are you talking about?" Her spine stiffened.

He casually buttoned his jacket. "I told you I thought it was excessive. You don't need all that cash at one time."

He was making it up. She didn't know why, but he was. "That never happened."

"The stress is getting to you." He managed to sound concerned as he said it.

"No." She held out a hand to fend him off when he tried to hug her. The motion proved useless when he pulled her into his arms.

"Victoria dear, it's okay."

She shook her head. "I didn't take the money."

"Of course you did." He brushed a hand over her hair as he pressed her face into his shoulder. "It's like the thing with the stove yesterday."

"I never turned it on." She knew she hadn't. He yelled at her for trying to burn the house down, but she had never even been into the kitchen.

He did it. Did it and wouldn't admit it.

The countless scenes played over and over in her head. So many things he insisted happened or didn't. So many facts she knew were wrong.

Something was happening to her. Something that took the reality she knew and twisted it into something sick.

"It was off when I left and on when I got back." He pulled back to look down at her. "It was a mistake. You can admit that you messed up."

"I didn't do it."

He sighed. "I really think you should see someone."

"This isn't about me. It's about you."

"You keep telling yourself that, but it's only a form of denial. You won't be able to go over this until you deal with it."

She gave him credit. In a way he was right. She had to confront the truth. "Where were you yesterday?"

"Work." His hands dropped to his sides. "We talked about this."

They hadn't. The night replayed clearly in her mind. She'd refused to talk when she suspected he'd been out sleeping with someone else. She'd heard the rumors. Saw women whisper behind their hands in the bathrooms of the clubs.

Call it denial, but she smelled the sickly sweet scent on him one time too many. Rather than face the argument she knew they had to have, rather than make the decision to end it, she'd pulled in tight.

That's how she knew this time he was definitely wrong about what transpired between them. Having that knowledge, she now started to question every time he insisted one thing happened when she believed another.

He had her so wound up and confused that she honestly didn't know what was happening to her. Until now.

This wasn't about depression or needing therapy. This was about him. He was playing a sick game that warped their relationship even further and threatened to drive her mad. She just wished she understood why.

He brushed a hand through his hair. "Why don't we—"

She backed away, putting as much room as possible between them. "No."

"Victoria."

"My name is Jennifer."

"It's whatever I say it is." His growl bounced off the walls, making her flinch.

She grabbed her purse. "I'm going to Heather's house."

"Running to your big sister. You're pathetic."

"I'm leaving." She rushed to the door, afraid he would try to stop her.

"Wait until you try to get back in here."

She spun around. Did a quick glance around the apartment and decided she could replace anything. Him, the furniture, even her paperwork. But if she didn't leave soon he would suck out her soul. "I'll be back later."

"Don't bother." He swept his hand over the kitchen table and knocked her empty glass to the floor. It shattered with an earsplitting crash against the hardwood. "You know what you are?"

His words stopped her hand from turning the knob. "An idiot for staying with you."

"You take off your clothes for money. There's only one definition for that type of work."

In two sentences he'd said all the accusations she feared when she took the Naked News job. "Don't say it."

"That makes you a whore. One I created. A pure invention of my imagination."

"*You* get out."

"Why should I? You don't have the strength to make it without me."

Backing down didn't calm him. Fighting just inflamed him. There wasn't a good choice, so she went with the truth. "At least I don't sleep around. That's you."

"Do you blame me?"

She refused to let his words slice and dice her. With her heart thudding and her mind buzzing with the possibility of a life without him. "You're a shadow of the man you once were. And, honestly, you weren't that great to begin with."

He pointed at her. "You will learn to obey me."

"Never."

"I will not let some whore try to run my life."

"I don't want to have anything to do with you."

He swore. "I guess you plan to run back to Paul. Now that he's finally called, you can beg him to take you back."

She blocked out his words. She couldn't let her mind go to Paul, or Preston would see the weakness and exploit it.

"Is that it, Victoria?" Preston took a step toward her.

She held up her hands but was prepared to do whatever it took if he even tried to touch her. "Stay away from me."

"All you've ever wanted was some construction guy from a small town."

It made her sick to think Preston had ever spent one second thinking about Paul. Preston wasn't good enough to wash Paul's clothes.

She slid to her left to get away from him and lost her balance. Her feet tangled beneath her and she went flying, air sucking past her as her face headed for the hard floor. At the last minute, she turned and landed with a groan on her shoulder.

Glass crunched under her. She couldn't remember where it came from, but it was in her hair and cutting into her palm. Her bones creaked and jaw rattled. She'd never seen stars before, but she made them out clearly in the darkness that fell over her eyes.

Preston crouched down with his face close to hers. "You can't do anything right."

When he stepped around her and walked out the door, she let out the jagged breath she'd been holding.

Two hours later, Jennifer scanned the concerned faces across from her on the couch. She sat bundled up in a throw and curled on a chair. "I'm fine."

Her best friend and true confidante, Andrea, stared back with hollow cheeks and flat lips. She wore her straight blonde hair in a ponytail, making her look years younger. They were ten years apart in age, but saw so many things the same way.

People mistook her quiet watchfulness for something else. One look in those soulful blue eyes and the intelligence behind them was obvious. The woman was a private investigator after all.

Jennifer depended on her friendship and missed spending time with her as Preston became more demanding and so insulting. And she had never seen her friend so serious or sad. She knew the worry was for her. The people she loved looked at her with a mix of concern and anger.

She recognized the emotions because they warred within her. "I panicked when I called you. I calmed down right after."

"You are not okay. You are a mess."

"I gotta agree with Andrea on this one." Andrea's husband, Will, glanced at Jennifer's hand and then to her face.

"It was a fight that got out of hand." Jennifer kept rising to Preston's defense. It was an ingrained reaction. One she couldn't seem to skip even when he scared the hell out of her.

Heather stood up. "Enough."

All eyes went to her.

Andrea rushed to diffuse the situation. "Heather, I don't think this is the time."

"He is an ass. He's been one for years, and you keep taking it. You are smarter than this. Walk away."

"Hey." Andrea demanded Jennifer's attention simply by shifting forward on the couch cushion and holding Jennifer's hands in her own. "We are all here for you."

"I want to move you out and hide you somewhere that idiot will never find you," Will mumbled.

Andrea did not take her gaze off of Jennifer. "What we want isn't the issue. This is about you. What you need."

Jennifer shook her head, lost in the pain of having her life run so far off course. "I don't know how I got here."

Heather closed her eyes. When she opened them again, the lashes were suspiciously wet. "You didn't do anything wrong."

Deep inside Jennifer knew that. She'd been beaten down but not destroyed. Preston had tried to wipe the Jennifer she knew off the planet and replace her with his vision of Victoria. He banged away, chipping at her self-confidence day by day while she let him take that level of control over her.

But she always reserved something for herself. She retreated in her memories and forged a path around him. She failed in some respects and she needed to own up to that, but she could turn everything around. Take control.

Jennifer stared at her hands, at anything but the caring eyes in front of her. She knew she'd disappointed them on some level. They would never say it, but it would take her a long time to recover from it.

Andrea squeezed Jennifer's hands. "He's threatened by you. By your success."

Will put a hand on his wife's shoulder. "She's right. Preston looks together but he's a complete—"

"He's unstable," Heather said.

"On the inside he's a little boy and you're this toy," Andrea said.

Jennifer couldn't help but laugh at that one. "Thanks."

Andrea smiled, but it lacked her usual warmth and charm. "You know what I mean. He doesn't respect you as a woman."

"He wants you to be how he sees you." Heather crossed her arms in front of her.

Jennifer glanced at the wall of concern and realized how lucky she was. These people cared about her. She called, and they dropped everything to come running. Will left work and Andrea wouldn't talk about the investigative assignment she was supposed to be working. They loved her unconditionally. As real love was supposed to be.

And they'd obviously been talking about her. "How long have you guys been saving all of this up?"

Will shrugged. "They talk about you all the time."

Andrea gave him the wifely evil eye she did so well. "You're not helping."

"Sorry."

Andrea shook her head. "The bottom line is you deserve better. I don't know exactly what he said or did, but I saw the one thing today I never wanted to see."

Jennifer had seen so many terrible things. She didn't even know how to start the list. "What?"

"You afraid." Andrea's words brought a fresh well of tears to Jennifer's eyes.

Will nodded. "You deserve so much more."

Jennifer loved Will for loving Andrea. Now she loved him for saying that. She could never imagine him calling her names. Andrea wouldn't tolerate it, but Will wasn't that guy. "You're a good man."

"And you will find one of your own."

"Preston isn't it." Heather added the comment as if they hadn't all already made that clear.

That was the one point Jennifer didn't need help to understand. "I know."

Heather's eyes widened. "You do?"

Will smiled. "Looks like she does."

"I'm not going to sit here and make excuses for his behavior." Jennifer let her feet fall to the floor and shrugged the blanket to the side. "But I do need your help."

"Anything." Andrea sat back into Will's waiting arm. "Will will hit him with a stick."

"Gladly."

"Tempting, but I think I know a better idea." Jennifer stood up. Fueled with their support, she could do this. Had to do this. "We need boxes."

Heather glanced around at all of them. "Excuse me?"

"We're packing up his stuff while he's out." Saying the words helped to heal the emotional wounds inside Jennifer. Knowing she had a plan was such a huge start. "The locksmith will be here in a few minutes."

Will threw his head back and laughed. It took him a full minute to get himself under control again. "Aren't you full of surprises."

Less than fifteen minutes later, she placed the call and told him where he could pick up his stuff.

He scoffed. "I'm on the lease."

"For now." She refused to be intimidated. Those days were gone. His suspected substance use could ruin her career, and he'd shown he didn't think twice about leaving her knocked out on the floor.

"You don't get to make decisions about my living arrangements." She could hear him shuffling papers. "I'll be home in an hour to discuss this in a rational manner."

If he came near her, she'd lose it. Not by bursting into tears but by laying into him. She was not going to be a victim for one more second. He could live in denial, but she wasn't going to. She would protect herself. "Come near me again and I will ruin your business reputation."

He called her a name. Swore in a vicious string that once would have slapped her flat.

This time the harsh words rolled off her. "And Preston? People will believe me."

She hung up.

Twenty-Four

*People have the ability to bring you great sorrow and
unbelievable joy. You need to experience both.*

—Grandma Gladys, The Duchess

GETTING HER LIFE TOGETHER WAS NOT AS SIMPLE AS
kicking Preston out. While her personal life shuffled under the
crumbling weight of a failed relationship, the world blew apart.
She stood in front of the camera one day and described the hor-
rors of 9/11. Suddenly she didn't understand where she fit in.

A strong therapist helped. So did the support of her friends and
family. But she needed something else. That was her only explanation for being in the bar this night.

She stood at the back of the dark hall with her hair in a ponytail, no makeup, and glasses. No one would ever mistake her for
Victoria Sinclair. Heck, she barely looked like Jennifer.

But slowly, she was finding her way back to the Jennifer she was
before Preston. A few seconds of seeing Paul helped. He sat at the
drums and pounded away, setting the beat and getting people up
on their feet. His hair took on the color of the shaded lights above
him as his arms pounded the air.

Sweaty and focused on something she didn't fully understand, he was still the most compelling man in the room. Being this close to him and not touching, not even saying hello, was pure torture.

This wasn't about her or connecting. She was broken and incomplete. Her life in shambles to the point she only now started looking at the pieces to see where they fit together again.

Taking the leave of absence from Naked News was a good first step. She associated the job with Preston. She'd nurtured it and earned the fame, but Victoria rose out of her time with him and she needed to heal from all of that. So she had to set it aside for awhile.

Once again their timing failed.

Going to Paul now, under those circumstances and with every part of her life in disarray, would only cause more pain. She'd inflicted enough of that on him already. She'd walked out on him more than once and only now understood the toll that must have taken on him. She kept searching, insisting she needed to grow. He did it on his own, without her.

The beat swelled and the crowd roared with approval. Hands flew into the air and people danced. He moved them.

She loved that. Loved that he'd found something that filled him with such deep satisfaction. The contentment was clear to look at him. His concentration so deep and total.

She remembered the days when he aimed all of that energy in her direction. Yet she knew in her heart that leaving him had been the right thing to do. They'd needed to grow and discover.

She wouldn't have had her career, and he might not have this. Still, seeing him separate from her and happy stung. More than that, it cramped her stomach and filled her with regret.

She watched him for a few more minutes, letting her gaze

lovingly roam over his face and trim body. Memorizing every inch as she silently said goodbye.

It sucked to find the love of your life at fifteen.

Paul sat on his couch with his legs balanced on the coffee table in front of him. The website on the laptop highlighted the best dive sites on the Canadian Atlantic. He'd tried most, but now he had his underwater camera. He could take the intense photos he'd been dreaming about.

"You on the Internet?" Neil dropped into the chair closest to the couch.

"Obviously."

"Have you checked out Naked News?"

Paul's hands froze over the keys. "Don't know what that is but I like the sound of it."

"It's basically what you think it is—naked women and news."

He'd seen naked women in magazines, real life, and movies. Why not in the news? "The world is a fine place."

Neil laughed. "You really never heard of it?"

"Nope."

"Do you have a life?"

"I don't watch television."

"It's on the Internet."

Paul guessed that was a distinction that mattered. Not to him, but to Neil. "Okay. Don't watch shows on there either. There's this thing called the outside world. I'm sure you've heard of it. You put on shoes and go, you know, outside."

"Did you miss the part where I said the women were naked?"

Paul had to admit his friend had a point. "Okay, yeah, that's worth a look."

"I watched a clip. There was this redhead." Neil whistled. "Damn, she was fine."

Neil didn't exactly have trouble finding women. He always seemed to have at least one following him around. "You paid for this?"

"No. Found it on a search."

"Bet Claire loved that." Claire was his newest girlfriend and the possessive type. The mere mention of a strip club once sent her over the edge of reason.

Paul liked to bring the topic up in front of her just to watch Neil squirm. Juvenile, yes, but great fun.

Neil's chest puffed up as he tipped back a beer. "What Claire doesn't know—"

"You won't get your butt kicked over."

Neil toasted him. "Exactly."

"Since it's weird for two guys to sit inside and look at naked women—"

"It is?"

Sure sounded like it to Paul. There were some things that should remain private or between couples. Guys together should stick to action movies. "That's what theaters are for."

"Never thought of it that way."

Paul didn't want to think about it at all. "How about we stick to the dive sites?"

"Right."

Jennifer sat on the Adirondack chair and watched the waves roll in. Being at Lake Orr calmed her. The first few weeks had been rough. As always, she could trace the discomfort and anger back to Preston. Well, to her decisions as far as Preston was concerned.

She's added his name to the deed to her precious cottage, the place that served as her greatest escape from reality. They never married, but it caused a legal wrangle. Her lawyer advised her to write a check and pay Preston off. Signing it hurt as much as if she had pledged it in blood.

But that was over. The memories of him here had been wiped clean. He no longer lingered in any part of her life. She heard about him making deals, and she stayed away. His life was no longer her business, to the extent it ever really was.

But her year of solitude was nearing an end. She'd started growing restless. In addition to enjoying the quiet, she spent her days taping books for the blind and working as a coordinator for an organization that placed developmentally disabled people in community living situations. It was fulfilling work. Good work. But she missed her real life and missed even more the people she loved during her extended absences.

She'd gained weight. Finally free to eat what she wanted and wear what she wanted, she chose comfortable. The pounds piled on right after. Her breasts had filled out. She considered that one of the pros.

Plastic surgery never appealed to her, but she could understand why people did it. The fuller figure served as one more way to break from Preston's hold. It also camouflaged her. People looking for Victoria Sinclair expected a firm body, not the one she had now.

She liked her life, or was starting to. One of the best parts of her day was about to come. Her interest in tarot card reading had grown. The cards were a work of art, each deck different and so rich. She wished she could draw and design her own set. Without that, she depended on her friend Tamare to guide her. Jennifer had worked in her shop part-time years ago, and their bond remained.

In the aftermath of Preston, Jennifer had called Tamare to reconnect. Last week, Tamare delivered news only she could say, because it came from the heart. Her message was simple: lose the weight because it will not get you where you need to go.

Jennifer understood the lesson. When she was ready, she would follow the advice.

The question for today was bigger. Jennifer had been reading her own cards and getting the same message. She tried to block it, ignore it. It was the last thing she needed.

Tamare walked around the side of the house. "Good afternoon."

They greeted each other warmly and took a few minutes to catch up. Tamare was even nice enough not to mention the weight that hadn't disappeared.

"Well?" she asked.

Jennifer didn't pretend to misunderstand. "I don't want this message."

"That's not how this works."

"I'm not ready."

"The universe knows when you're ready. Your head might take longer." Tamare placed the cards on the small table between the chairs.

Jennifer answered a few questions, the whole time hoping she'd made a mistake.

Tamare looked up. "A man is coming for you."

Jennifer's stomach bounced up to her throat. "That can't be—"

"You can deny it if you want, but he's on the way. The question is if you'll be ready."

Jennifer already knew the answer to that one. "No."

Being alone was the worst. At night his mind would wonder and he'd start thinking about what could have been. How he couldn't commit to Wendy or any other woman. How the one who played the starring role in his dreams was the same one he hadn't seen in years.

Paul rolled over for what had to be the thirtieth time. He slammed his hand into his pillow and dragged the covers higher on his shoulder. When that failed, he flopped on his back.

His mind raced. He doubted Jennifer would even remember him. God knew the last conversation had been awkward. He knew what Preston wanted and fought back the need to agree.

The only thing that stopped him from ignoring common sense and taking the one thing he could get from her was the sound of her voice over the phone during that last call. She sounded so haunted. So lost. It killed him.

He closed his eyes.

Ten seconds later they popped open.

Maybe naked women and the news would help. Neil insisted the redhead was pretty nice looking.

Paul leaned over and flicked on the light. Dragging his laptop off the floor took a few more minutes, especially since he didn't bother climbing out of bed. It took another minute for the computer to fire up. Another few seconds to search for the site.

Then his fun crashed. The thing cost money? He had to subscribe? Hell, he probably should have figured that out, but Neil could have warned him.

Paul wasn't one to pay for sexual enjoyment. The closest he got to that kind of thrill was buying tickets to a hockey game. He dropped his head back against the headboard and closed his eyes, but they refused to stay shut.

· "Fine." He found the free trial link and clicked the keys. A pretty blonde popped up talking about the weather. "I could get used to this."

On second thought, maybe this wasn't the best show to put a guy to sleep. He felt more awake and keyed up now than he did a minute ago. He went to the next clip.

Jennifer's face appeared on his screen. A flashier version of Jennifer, maybe. This one under the name Victoria Sinclair.

He blinked a few times, expecting her to disappear. The only thing that dropped was her shirt. He'd recognize that body any-where. He'd spent hours exploring it. The rest didn't fit.

The date was from a few years before. He remembered seeing her in that wig and the change in her hair. Still, it didn't make sense. Her job had something to do with events.

He turned the volume up. There it was. The husky drawl that tickled his brain even after all this time. "Jennifer."

She kept talking. Kept taking off her clothes.

He didn't know if he should be excited or confused. He went with turned on and turned the light off.

Twenty-Five

When opportunity knocks, kick the door down.

—Grandma Gladys, The Duchess

SHE'D BEEN ON A LEAVE OF ABSENCE FOR MORE THAN a year when the call came from Walt. The show had taken a different direction while she was gone, and it wasn't working. Walt and the new guys leading the show wanted to bring the broadcast back to its original purpose. Not comedy or something bawdy. Simply pretty women delivering the news as they lost their clothes.

With months of thinking and hibernating behind her, she reluctantly left the safety of Lake Orr and headed back to the city. This wasn't just about an interview. She needed to come back to life. The cottage gave her peace, but it wasn't the real world. She didn't need to hide. Not anymore.

Heather offered the extra bedroom in her apartment, and Jennifer didn't refuse. Will and Andrea would be close by. So would Tamare. Her safety net would be secure.

She walked into the Naked News offices in her favorite black pants and red blouse. The color showed off her skin tone, but the outfit didn't hide the extra weight. Rather than try to ignore it, she decided to take responsibility for it. With the stress gone and the black cloud that hovered over her life dissipated, it would come off.

As she pushed open the glass doors to the conference room, she expected conflicting emotions. She'd left because she had to get out. The terms were good, and Walt understood, but she had worried all the old feelings of desperation would come rushing back on her.

They didn't. It was clear the negative thoughts she had of the place stemmed from Preston. With him gone, the burden lifted. Entering now, she remembered only the fun.

She slid into the seat the new secretary pointed for her. Across from her, Walt gave her a warm smile. The other guys didn't look as pleased. They were image consultants of some sort. They didn't work at Naked News. They supposedly knew business and were there to help get it right.

The board hired them for a short-term contract. Walt seemed to be tolerating them but just barely. She thought of them as Blondie and Big Shoulders and didn't like them on sight.

"You've been away for a long time," Blondie, the young one in the gray suit, stated.

"A year."

He glanced up and down her torso. "You look different from your tapes."

She'd gotten to a point in her life where verbal games annoyed her. "You mean heavier."

"Honestly? Yes."

Walt frowned. "Is that necessary?"

Big Shoulders nodded. "It's a concern if she wants to work here again."

In that second she wasn't sure she did. "Not to state the obvious, but you called me. I didn't come begging for work."

"I'm sorry?"

Jennifer took a long look at Big Shoulders. He was older, with less hair and shoulders that nearly swallowed his head. He struck Jennifer as the type of guy who thought nothing of assessing a woman's looks despite how wanting his own might be.

"I didn't ask to come back." She had no intention of returning until she'd heard Walt's voice on the phone asking for her to at least consider it. They'd noted her status as being on temporary leave, but in her head it had always been a final end.

"I understand you need work," Blondie said. "We can help you with that."

The guy acted like he was doing her a favor. Like she'd been spending her days sitting by the phone, just hoping Naked News would call so she could beg for a second chance.

Wrong.

"I think there's been a misunderstanding." She said the words slow, making sure she had their joint attention.

"How so?" Big Shoulders asked in a voice so like Preston's that Jennifer winced when she heard it.

"Walt called me and asked for my help."

Walt nodded. "True."

"He mentioned a slide in the ratings and thought I might be able to help you. Not the other way around."

Blondie shrugged. "We have other anchors."

Jennifer weighed her options. Sitting there, taking this and hanging around as if she needed them in order to survive might be the one avenue they wanted her to take, but she wasn't interested. She'd been down that road before and wasn't ready to trade one problem with another.

Big Shoulders clicked the end of his pen about fifty times. Once everyone stared at him, he spoke. "Before we can discuss terms, we need to talk about the weight."

Walt winced at the harsh comment.

Jennifer knew the feeling. Yes, the extra pounds magnified on television. Not exactly a secret. But there had to be a better way to deliver the message. A little tact would be nice.

"I've been on leave. The weight will come off now that I'm back here." She knew that was the case. She'd never been a sedentary person. She enjoyed the outside and exercise. Now that her mind had healed her body could, too.

Big Shoulders switched to tapping his pen against his front teeth. Another annoying habit as far as Jennifer was concerned. "Until we see some weight loss we could put you on an exercise program and offer discounted pay."

They could kiss her butt.

She stood up. "Gentlemen, while I appreciate you thinking of me, I'm going to pass."

Blondie glanced at Walt and then rushed to fill the conversation void. "I don't think you understand. This is a perfect opportunity for you to re-enter the public eye."

"It will take some sacrifices from you," said the other one.

These two were clueless. "I've sacrificed. And, believe me, I know what this position entails. I invented it."

Blondie's smarmy face went white. "What are you saying?"

"No thanks."

Walt showed up at her apartment two days later. When he called and asked if he could stop by, she didn't hesitate. Saying no to the deal had been the right answer. The guys at that table wanted another version of Preston's Victoria, the type they could push around. She wouldn't go back on those terms.

She had other opportunities. She'd been working since high school, even through college. Finding employment had never been an issue. She had experience and gave a good interview. She'd rebuilt and reinvested before and would do it again.

Making the decision had given her a sense of peace. She didn't realize how much she missed the calm certainty of life until she lost it and found it again.

She opened the door on the first knock. "That meeting was fun."

Walt didn't say a word, he just stepped inside and hugged her. "I'm sorry about that."

"Wasn't your fault." Jennifer knew that. Walt had never been anything but fair with her.

"They're the consulting guys. They don't understand how to run the show. I doubt they even know anything about the show or the demographics."

"Not the most tactful bunch ever." She still wanted to poke both of their eyes out.

"They're supposed to be so smart."

A chuckle burst out of her. "They hid that well."

When Walt joined her in laughter she knew everything was fine between them. With her arm in his, she lead him to the kitchen and mothered him with a hot cup of coffee and a muffin. Baking was one of her weaknesses now, and she was determined to share her skills.

Walt glanced around. "Where's Preston?"

"Long gone."

"Good."

"You weren't a fan?"

"Of you? Always." Walt took a sip of coffee. "Of how he treated you? No."

She didn't know what to say. She let her heart do it for her. "Thank you."

Walt nodded. "I thought we could try this negotiating thing again."

"Without the condescending crap."

"I'd like to think so."

The last of her anxiety eased. "How is your wife?"

He smiled. "I see what you're doing."

"What?"

"Uh-huh." He took a folded piece of paper out of his inner jacket pocket. "I won't be sidetracked. We'll get to the personal stuff once we finish up the business."

She admired his persistence. "I already said no."

"You're a smart businesswoman. Not one to turn down a good opportunity when it lands on your lap."

"Flattery will get you . . ." She reached for the basket in the middle of the table. "Another muffin."

"I'd rather have your signature." He slid the paper across the table to her. "Here's the offer."

She was almost afraid to look down. Turning down two strangers had been easy. Saying no to Walt would be harder. But she'd do it if she had to. For the first time, she knew in her heart Naked News needed her more than she needed it.

She peeked at the bottom line. A raise and a list of benefits she'd tried to negotiate in the past.

Nice.

She wanted to squeal, but she settled for ribbing him a bit. "What about the lower pay until the weight comes off?"

He took a big bite of muffin. "These are good." Then another. "And I know you. You'll lose the weight when you're ready."

Jennifer couldn't help but smile. Now that's how a tactful guy did it. "I will."

"Then as far as I'm concerned you deserve the salary increase now."

She broke off a piece of muffin. "You have a pen?"

"Sign so we can talk about family stuff."

Twenty-Six

A man is coming for you.

—Tarot reading

SIX WEEKS LATER, JENNIFER HAD LOST THE WEIGHT. A little exercise and a good metabolism accounted for the big change in such a short period of time. She didn't starve herself like she had in the Preston years. Never again.

She truly believed being happy and satisfied and not looking to food for a release helped. She also believed women should be happy with their bodies, and if that meant her weight settled out higher than before, she would have been fine with that.

Being pounded with work likely played a role too. As part of her new deal, she took over the public relations job at the network. She liked the addition of something new. It meant less time on-air but more time in administration. The shift in balance suited her.

It was also the reason she sat at her home office on a Sunday, looking through a mass of e-mails forwarded by Walt. He was the big boss. He sent PR-related stuff to her to handle. Getting used to the new position meant learning everything in steps. She checked all e-mails in case one was *the one* she had to handle immediately.

She clicked through a list and saw one Walt just forwarded. He tended to save Sundays for family, so she figured this one meant something.

She opened it and took a brief glance at something that looked like fan mail. Those pieces rarely came directly to her. She got enough to bury herself in it. The avalanche went to customer service, who waded through it and separated the general fan mail from personal stuff and the crazy ones.

The idea that Walt took the time to forward it stunned her. He was a busy man. And why to her?

She breezed through the header and stopped. The song she'd been singing along to on the radio stuck on an endless loop in her head. She actually touched her fingertips against the screen as if she could feel the words and hold them forever.

Hello Victoria, I don't know if you remember me, it's Paul Gobits from Sarnia. Congratulations on your exciting job. It's been years and it would be nice to catch up. I am playing at the El Macombo in Toronto on Tuesday March 24th, it would be great if you could stop by and say hello.

Paul. Just seeing his name sent blood spinning through her veins. She wanted to scream with joy and throw her fists in the air.

He'd found her. Paul being Paul, he didn't ask dumb questions or judge. His e-mail was filled with an open charm and a simple question. She admired the directness of it. If she'd tried to get in touch with him first, something she thought about on a daily basis, she would have taken weeks composing and revising until it was perfect.

She reached over and shut off the radio. "Heather!"

Jennifer didn't wait for her sister to hit the room to start typing a reply. There was no need to hesitate. She was at the point in her life where seeing Paul made her nervous and giddy, not fearful or worried.

Heather peeked around the corner. "What is wrong with you?"

"Paul e-mailed me."

"Paul?"

"Paul."

"Get out." She hovered over Jennifer's shoulder and read the original and then the finished lines of the draft reply. "You're going, right?"

"We are." She'd taken huge steps forward, but that didn't mean she couldn't get hit with panic now and then.

"What are you doing right now?"

Jennifer's fingers flew across the keys. Typing 130 words per minute came in handy sometimes. "Saying yes."

"Stop a second."

"No way."

"Listen to me." Heather brushed Jennifer's hands off the keyboard.

"What the—"

"Don't."

Jennifer couldn't believe it. Heather knew the truth. Knew everything about Paul and the history. "Why?"

"Just show up."

Whatever Jennifer was about to write left her head. "Really?"

"You look amazing. Your life is together. From everything I've heard, so is his."

"You heard about him?"

Heather waved the question away. "Trust me on this. Your big sister wouldn't steer you wrong."

Jennifer nibbled on her bottom lip. "Really?"

"You've always said your greatest regret was losing him, that your timing was off." Heather smiled. "This time you can make it happen."

"You're matchmaking."

Heather shrugged. "Who knows? Maybe this time it will stick."

The location of their first meeting in years impressed the heck out of Jennifer. The club, El Macombo, was a famous live music joint in Toronto. The Rolling Stones and other famous bands had stopped by unannounced for jam sessions. The idea of Paul being there, playing there, filled her with a ferocious pride. The achievement was his, but she gloried in the fact he had gotten there. No one handed him an easy life. If he'd made it here, he'd earned it.

Dressing for the night was only one in a long line of problems. Hard to know what to wear to see the love of your life for the first time in years. Even harder when the email issued a casual invitation.

Jennifer didn't know if Paul wanted to introduce her to his new wife or something else. Every time her mind traveled to the first possibility, her stomach rebelled.

Then there was the problem of being noticed. Ever since Naked News had been picked up by a local station, it was harder for her to be Jennifer in public. Heather and her boyfriend agreed to tag along for protection and moral support. Jennifer vowed to duck behind them if a drunk fan got out of hand.

The slim-fitting electric blue shirt and blue jeans were perfect for the bar, at least she hoped so. She hadn't been in a club or bar in a year. Preston ruined those haunts for her.

When they walked in, the place was almost empty due to the early hour. The main crowd would pile in to hear the music a few hours from now.

"Where is he?" Heather asked.

Jennifer looked around. No band in sight. The only people in the room were the bartender and the sound mixer. Both were busy with their respective jobs.

"I could ask someone," she said more to herself than for agreement.

"It's your show."

Jennifer ignored Heather's comment and walked over to the sound guy. "Do you know Paul Gobits?"

The guy didn't look up. "Sure."

Maybe being noticed wouldn't be such a bad thing. Might mean better service. "Can you clue me in to his current location?"

This time he glanced up. He must have liked what he saw because a smile broke across his face. A second later, he pointed behind her.

She turned in time to see Paul come out of the prep room. He walked in and stopped right under a pool of light. The haze circled his head, making him look like an angel. An angel with broad shoulders and the soft hair she remembered so well.

Her hungry gaze ran over him. The blue jeans and tee hugged his trim frame. Tall and fit without a wedding ring.

She took it all in during a short flash no longer than a blink. When her stare returned to his face, he was looking at her and smiling.

Her heart leapt. Took a jump and landed right in her throat. It pounded hard enough to break through her skin. She had no idea how she would talk. She wanted to throw her body at him, wrap her arms and legs around him and never let him go.

He moved before she did. One second he was standing there like a figure out of her dreams, and the next he took two steps and landed in front of her.

He put out his hand and then held onto hers as he beamed that sexy smile in her direction. "If it isn't Jennifer Hopkins."

"Paul Gobits."

He dropped her hand but didn't move back. "I didn't think you'd come."

Little did he know she almost ran the whole way there. Only Heather's insistence stopped that little escapade. "Why?"

"I expected you to send a representative to make sure I wasn't some kind of wacko."

She couldn't stop smiling. Her cheeks actually hurt from the force of it. "Are you?"

He quirked an eyebrow. "Not usually."

That quickly, she felt at ease. All those worries about timing and him being with someone else fell by the wayside. Comfort came with the welcoming warmth in his eyes.

"You do know you're famous, right?" he asked.

She never thought of it in those terms. "I'm still Jennifer Hopkins from Sarnia."

"You always will be to me."

It never failed. He said the right thing at the right time and sent her stomach tumbling. "Do you have time to sit down and talk?"

He glanced at the clock behind the bar. "About a half hour and I'm all yours."

They sat down, and he signaled the bartender for a drink. "I keep thinking this is a dream."

"For me, too."

She tore slices in the napkin she twirled between her fingers. It was either that or throw her arms around his neck and hug him close enough to feel his heartbeat against hers. "So you're still playing music."

"And you're still beautiful."

"Sweet talker."

His smile reached the whole way to his beautiful eyes. "Sounds like you've been busy in the years since we last saw each other."

The way he said it, amused and without judgment, put her at ease. "You have no idea."

"Tell me."

"It's not all that interesting."

He took one of her hands in his. "I want to know everything about you. Every minute and every dream. It all matters to me."

"Do I get to hear the same from you?" She remembered how closed he'd been, how secretive.

He lifted their joint hands and kissed her knuckles. "Ask anything."

"That's a pretty open invitation."

"Whatever you want is yours."

All the past tension was gone. He didn't panic or tense when she turned her attention on him. He opened the door and dared her to walk through it.

She did. At the end of thirty minutes she knew all about his photography interests and scuba trips. He didn't talk about a girl-friend, and she didn't ask. Hearing it on his lips would bury her in grief all over again.

The strange news was his address. He lived only four blocks away from her. All that time and so close.

A man is coming for you.

The longer they talked, the more she wanted the press of his body against hers, the taste of his lips against hers. It was as if they were transported back to the good times. Like they'd never been apart or with other people.

Every part of her silently screamed with joy. Seeing him was a gift she never expected to receive. Being this close, sliding her thigh against his as they sat there, reinforced her view that sometimes people did get lucky.

She wanted more . . . and this time the more in question was him.

The room filled around them, and the sound guy motioned for Paul to come up to the stage. She didn't want the time to end. No way was she letting him slip out of sight and out of her life again.

"Can you come over on Friday?" She rushed out the question before he walked away. Any day worked for her, but choosing a weekend day worked as a test. She wanted to know if he was available.

"I can do Saturday."

He returned the volley with ease. Didn't give any extra information about his Friday plans to put her mind at rest. She would have to stumble through the week, waiting to see him. But none of that made any difference. She felt lighter, her nerve endings singing and shouting with excitement.

When he stood up to get ready for his set, she almost grabbed his hand again. Letting him go proved as hard this time as it had in the past, and she knew this separation was only temporary.

"You going to stick around and listen?" He asked the question before he walked away.

She motioned to the bar. "Heather and her boyfriend would be upset if I dragged them the whole way here only to take them away without hearing any music."

Paul waved to Heather. "Man, I didn't even see them."

4

He'd been too busy looking at her. Jennifer knew the truth and reveled in it.

"I think we'll refrain from letting Heather know that," Jennifer said.

"She'd kick my butt, and I'd deserve it." Paul tucked a loose strand of hair behind her ear and leaned so close that his warm, fragrant breath tickled her skin. "Enjoy the show."

She already had.

Twenty-Seven

Only forward.

—Jennifer Hopkins

THE DAYS TICKED BY FOR WHAT FELT LIKE WEEKS. Paul thought he would go crazy waiting for Saturday to arrive. He immediately regretted testing Jennifer.

Delaying seeing her for an extra day seemed like a good idea at the time. He didn't want to seem pathetic, but now he wished he'd been honest about not having another date. He didn't want anyone else. Sure didn't want another day to pass without touching her.

Jennifer opened the door before he could knock. "Hi."

"Hi."

She nodded. "I'm thinking that's enough talk for now."

Heat flashed through him. "Where's Heather?"

"Not here."

"Any chance I can come inside?"

Jennifer laughed in a sound filled with warmth. "I think we've played this scene before."

"I am dying to hold you, kiss you, and I'm happy to do it right here in the hallway, but your neighbors might get testy."

She threw her arms around his neck and sealed his mouth with hers. It was one of those mind-blowing kisses that whipped through him, wiping out every bad memory and replacing them with a sizzling need.

He groaned against her lips. "I missed you so much."

He didn't care who saw them or heard them. How much ego he had to set aside to get this time right. The entire building could come out and watch, and she could post his feelings for her on the broadcast. Nothing was going to drive him away. Not this time.

"Come inside." She took his hand and led him through the sunny front room.

He expected her to drag him to the couch. They passed the beige sectional, then the table. They were at the base of the stairs and up before he could blink.

With every step, his body's alert status rose. Seeing her bedroom door and the mattress beyond stole his speech. He'd expected talk and a getting-to-know-you-again phase. She was offering so much more.

The fast forward proved what he thought at the club—they didn't need to go backward. They could spin right into the future.

He ran his fingers through her hair and felt her tremble. He smelled flowers on her skin and gave in to the need to trail his fingers down her back. She shifted her head to the side to give him better access.

It was all the incentive he needed.

He pressed her back against the bedroom door and trapped her there between his arms. "You sure you're ready?"

She lifted her lower body against his. "I've been waiting all week."

"I thought about sleeping on your doorstep until you let me in."

He wrapped her hair around his finger, letting the silky strands fall over his skin.

"I would have dragged you through a window to get you to the bedroom." She whispered the sexy threat against his lips before dragging him into another kiss. "Like I basically just did."

He nuzzled her cheek then her nose. "I want to go slow and re-learn all the things you enjoy."

She reached for the buttons on his shirt. "Next time."

They didn't even try to talk until almost two hours later. In bed, naked and lounging on the rumpled sheets, she celebrated the special moment. For all the times they got this wrong, this time it felt right. All the heartbreak was behind them.

The usual panic didn't overtake her. She wasn't worried about growing up and growing apart. Thoughts of losing herself and her dreams didn't take hold. She'd lived enough to know he was her every fantasy.

All she wanted to do was hold on and not let go.

She propped her shoulders on the only remaining pillow on the bed. Paul held his body over hers as he brushed his fingertips against the bare skin above her breasts.

"Please tell me you're not seeing anyone." She knew he wasn't, that he wouldn't do that to her, but she needed to hear the words. The implicit promise would be enough.

He pretended to mull over the question until she pinched the skin on his elbow. "I have a rotating harem, but I gave them the night off."

"You're such a good guy."

"I prefer the term master."

She threw her head back and laughed. "I bet you do."

His lips found her exposed neck and began nibbling. "No."

"What?"

"There's only you." He pressed his index finger in the sweet spot between her eyebrows.

All the tension in her body fled. "And only you for me."

Light kisses fell in a line along her collarbone. Soft hair tickled her neck as warm breath skimmed across her skin.

She turned her head to give him better access. "I can't believe you e-mailed me."

"I saw you on television and . . ." He shook his head. "Never mind. Doesn't matter."

It did when he said it like that. "What?"

"Well, I waited for a long time before getting in touch. I worried you were with someone else or wanted to forget our time together."

"I've never forgotten you. I've lived on those memories for years."

His forehead pressed against her shoulder. "I love you." The soft whisper skipped over her skin.

Everything fell together. Every jagged edge smoothed. "Paul."

He shook his head but didn't look at her. "It's too soon, I know. Neil told me to play it cool. I planned to hold it, but seeing you here, in my arms . . ."

She pressed her hands against his cheeks and forced him to look at her. "I love you, too. Always have."

It felt good to finally say the words. Freeing and so permanent. She'd never uttered them to anyone else because they never fit. They were reserved for him and him alone.

Still, the delay seemed interminable. "Why did we wait so long?" She was the one to ask, knowing full well that any blame belonged to her. He'd tried to hold them together, but she pushed them apart. All of her reasons were valid. They weren't ready, and pushing forward prematurely probably would have killed them for the long-term.

It all made sense to her, but that didn't mean he saw it the same way. If his bitterness still lingered, it would surround them until it crushed them.

"Paul?"

"It was a long road. Sometimes pretty awful, but we're here." His eyes were clear and his voice steady.

She knew he was telling the truth. On this one point, they were in sync. "And now?"

"I'm not leaving."

"Me either." She stretched, hoping to tempt him into a second round by sliding out of the sheet and showing a bit more skin. "Guess that means you like what you saw on the Naked News video."

She expected him to joke. Instead, his smile faded.

"For the record, I like Victoria. She's hot and fun and very sexy." He traced her mouth. "But I love Jennifer. Only Jennifer. The rest can come or go, you can make money or we can struggle to pay the bills, being with Jennifer is my only focus."

Light poured through her, illuminating all the previously dark places. He got it. "So many people can't see the difference."

"Then they don't know you."

"You do."

His mouth kicked up at one side. "And I like it all."

She lifted her hands over her head and flashed him her wildest come-get-me grin. "Show me."

"Thought you might actually like to see the house," Jennifer said.

He was fine limiting his access to the bedroom for now, but the next morning he followed Heather and Jennifer through the two-story apartment, listening as they described the rooms. He didn't see any of it. Jennifer held his hand, and the feel of her skin blocked out all of his powers of concentration.

"You look ready to bolt," Heather joked.

"I'm fine." He kissed Jennifer. "Great, actually."

Jennifer smiled . . . then it faded. "Where's Luna?"

He knew she was talking English but the words didn't make much sense. "What is a Luna?"

"My dog."

The idea made sense. She loved animals. "I didn't see her last night."

And he remembered everything—the scent of her skin and curve of her spine. Not one memory of a fuzzy dog.

All of the color leeched out of Heather's face. "Oh no."

"What?" he asked.

Jennifer stared at her sister. "She wouldn't."

"Anyone want to fill me in?"

The sisters took off for the stairs, screaming as they ran. He followed because the curiosity was killing him. They ran across the hardwood floor, sliding in their socks as they hit the dining room doorway.

"Luna!"

Paul took in the whole scene. Bits of food scattered on the floor. Broken dishes. A dog happily munching on what looked like the remainder of a piece of turkey.

Jennifer shook her finger in front of the dog's face. "Bad girl."

Paul ruined the scolding by laughing. The scene was just so perfect. This forty pound ball of fluff had helped herself to a full brunch buffet. He shook until he doubled over.

"This isn't funny. She ate all the cheese." Jennifer crouched down to peek under the table. "I think she even ate the lettuce. Is that possible?"

Her disgruntled confusion only made him laugh harder.

"You won't think it's funny when she has to go out in the middle of the night."

That one sobered him. "I'll take her."

Jennifer eyed him up. "You plan to be here?"

He saw the words for the challenge they were. She wanted a commitment, an understanding of some sort. With other women, he balked. With her, he couldn't say yes fast enough. "I will be here for as long as you let me."

She stepped over a wayward strip of bacon and wrapped her arms around his neck. "I like that."

He wasn't going to rush and start thinking about moving in together. He'd done that once and watched her slip away.

"You invite me and I'll be here." Catching her in his arms felt right. They fit together, his hard body sliding so perfectly against her softness.

"The invitation is forever."

But he wasn't going to say no when she offered up his dream and asked him to take it. "Good."

Twenty-Eight

There's always a way.

—Jennifer Hopkins

"Boston."

They stood on the back patio of her house the next night, watching the people pass by as the sun faded on the horizon. He slid his arms around her waist and pulled her back against him. "That's his name."

"Is he a friendly dog or a sloppy dog?"

He kissed her shoulder. "What do you mean by sloppy?"

"You know."

"Actually, no. But you'll love him. He's a Rottweiler."

She smiled against his cheek. "Of course he is."

"I remember that day." The sunshine. The blinding clarity that he would never feel that way with another person.

"I've held onto it in my mind through all the tough times."

He adjusted his hold to pull her even closer. "You want to tell me about those?"

She nodded. "Soon."

"I can wait for as long as you need."

233

She pressed her elbow into his stomach. "You're just changing the subject. About this dog . . ."

"He's good. Well, there was this one time."

"Uh-oh."

"He attacked another dog."

She turned around in his arms to face him. "And this dog sleeps with you? You think he's going to sleep on our bed?"

He loved it when she said *our* bed. "He's harmless."

"I bet the other dog didn't think so."

"He was this husky. Mean."

"Like that one." She waved to the man walking his dog by the patio wall.

Paul felt his eyes bulge. "Jennifer."

She kept waving, drawing as much attention to them as possible. "Hi Mango!"

"That's him."

Her head snapped back around. "What?"

He tried to drag her back against the wall and out of the line of sight. "That's him. That's him."

"What are you doing?"

"Boston attacked that dog." Paul pointed in the direction of the retreating man as he spoke.

She slapped a hand over her mouth. "Are you kidding?"

"Hardly."

Laughter bubbled out and over her hand. "That was your dog?"

The anxiety inside him calmed to a steady boil. "How do you know the story?"

"Everyone knows the story. Mango's owner told everyone who would listen. He made Boston out to be a vicious killer."

Paul felt outraged on Boston's behalf. "Who is this guy?"

"The dog's owner? He's my photographer."

Paul's lungs deflated. "Well, damn."

She doubled over. It took another few minutes before she regained her composure and could talk without losing it again. "The real question is, with how our lives have connected and how close we live together, how we didn't cross paths before that email you sent."

The last of his worries fled. Here he was worried about pets and stupid neighborhood issues and she was concentrating on their lives together. On a potential relationship. Speaking in terms of them and never just her.

He liked the way her mind was working. "We always did have a case of chronically bad timing."

She shook her head. "Not anymore."

A man stepped right in front of her near the front of the deli. He was older, maybe in his late fifties, and from the way his T-shirt rode up on his belly, looked like he'd eaten more than his share of desserts.

He pointed at her. "You're that woman."

She hated this part. The overly friendly bordering on combative meetings with people who had seen her on the Internet. Most of her fan meetings were positive, but every now and then, one wandered into danger territory. This guy didn't seem dangerous, and there were people around and clerks in the store, but he seemed like the entitled-to-touch type. Her least favorite.

"Excuse me." She tried to maneuver around him.

He stepped closer until less than a body width separated them. "The one who strips on the TV."

She didn't bother to correct him. Instead, she tried to slip back and ran smack into the magazine display. Glancing around, she picked out Paul's back on the other side of the room. He was facing away from her, saying something to the man at the counter as he got out his wallet to pay.

The older man stepped into her line of sight. "Hey, don't be shy. I like the show. I really like you."

"You have me confused—"

"How about a kiss?" The man reached out to touch her.

Paul shoved the other man's hand away and executed the perfect body block. "What do you think you're doing?"

"Just saying hello to the lady. You can wait your turn." The man tried to look around Paul.

Paul held his ground. "The lady is with me."

The man laughed. "Man, she's with everyone. Have you seen her on TV?"

Tension pulsed off Paul. "Get out of here."

"It's okay." She grabbed the back of his shirt. Gathered up a big wad in her fist and tried to tug him closer. He didn't budge.

"Yeah, Paul. The lady is happy with me." The man smiled at her. "See?"

"I don't know where the hell you learned your manners, but they're rusty. This is a lady, and you don't touch a lady without her permission. Got it?" Paul didn't close in or raise a hand to the guy, but the deadly tone to his voice said it all.

"She's not—"

Paul cleared his throat. "One more word and we settle this outside."

She yanked the material even tighter in her hand. "Paul!"

"Hey, man. Just trying to talk to her. Tell her I'm a fan."

She couldn't see Paul's face, but she saw this guy's. The color drained right out of him. Something in the way Paul stood or talked or looked got through.

"Write her a letter." Paul reached around and slipped an arm around her. "Let's go."

They were halfway down the block before she stopped shaking. It took another block before she could say anything. "I'm sorry."

Paul's eyebrows slid together as he frowned. "Why are you apologizing?"

She fiddled with her hands, rubbing them together and then linked her fingers to keep from flipping them all around. "Scenes like that don't happen very often, but every now and then a guy goes too far."

"And when he does, I'll be there to stop it."

"I know it's hard."

Paul slowed his pace. "What?"

"Dealing with what I do."

This time he stopped. With his hand on her elbow, he gently pulled her out of the way of sidewalk traffic and brought her up against the concrete building to his right. "Hold on a second."

"I just—"

"Jennifer, look at me." He waited until she did before talking again. "If you have a problem with what you do, then let's talk about that. But don't assume I do. I'm not that guy."

"I know that."

"Then what's the problem?"

She blew out the heavy breath tucked in her chest. "We never talked about it. The Victoria thing, I mean. Other men seeing me. I don't know how you feel about it."

To her, the decision made sense. She'd gone from being led around by someone else to making her own decisions. Coming back to Naked News on her terms gave her strength. For so long she'd talked about women being in control of their bodies and their decisions, and now she was.

But that was a life she chose on her own, when her decisions affected only her. Now she had Paul to consider. She planned to make a life with him. This time they could unload the baggage of the past and concentrate on a future. So long as he understood her choices and didn't judge them.

True, he hadn't been anything but supportive, but she didn't know how much a guy could handle. He was better than most—the best, actually—but many would deplore the idea of other men seeing their woman naked. It would feed their insecurities and concerns until it destroyed them.

She couldn't do that to Paul. To them.

"You know what I see when I watch you deliver the news?"

That was her concern. "No."

"A smart and capable businesswoman. You saw a niche and created Victoria to fill it."

She couldn't let him think the outlook she had now, the positive way she viewed the job and her body, was how it had always been. She'd shared with him about parts of her life with Preston, even the hard ones near the end. She talked about the lack of self-confidence and pain in losing her soul.

In time, she'd tell it all. Until then, she needed him to understand that Victoria rose from a dark place. Maybe she walked in the light now, but she was a reminder of something difficult, too. "Other people created her. Preston would say he made her."

"Preston is an ass."

"I'm not going to argue with that."

"Victoria comes from you." Paul pressed his palm against her chest, right over her thumping heart. "From here. She wouldn't exist without you, and if someone tells you something else, send them to me."

Being with him made her feel safe and cherished. "I like that you're protective."

He ran the backs of his fingers down her cheek. "What I am is in love with you. All of you. All parts. All of the pieces."

"Victoria is an act." One she'd perfected to the point where it almost took over everything else. Pulling back from that edge had been hard, nearly impossible. She could not let that line blur again.

"She's in you." He touched her nose. "But she's not you." His fingers trailed down her throat.

She hadn't experienced any doubts since finding him again, but she had worried about not being able to live up to the image he had of her in the past. Worse, of not being able to overcome it. With the soft look in his eyes and the husky tone in his sure voice, her last bit of panic faded away.

He understood her, really saw her for who she was and what she wasn't. The love didn't come with conditions or an expiration. "No one has ever understood me before."

"Because you weren't with the right guy then."

"I am now."

He kissed her. "Definitely."

Twenty-Nine

Right woman. Right time.

—Paul Gobits

PAUL SAT IN HIS FAVORITE LAWN CHAIR AND LOOKED out over the water of Lake Orr. Boston and Luna romped in the yard, smelling something particularly interesting by the tree and ignoring the humans.

Jennifer had spent the afternoon cooking something with barley. He didn't care what its name was because he wasn't eating it. She could mix up whatever mash-up of vegetables and grains she wanted, he'd stick with corn.

"For you." She handed him a glass of iced tea then slid into the chair beside him.

"You are the perfect woman."

"And flattery will get you anything."

He let his hands drop against the armrests. "I'm still recovering from last night."

She smiled at him over the rim of her glass. "I think we traumatized the dogs."

"They've seen worse."

"I wonder how much doggy therapy costs."

240

"You are talking about animals that sniff each other's butts. Anything we do is tame in comparison."

The breeze grabbed her hair, so she tucked the strands behind her ears. "There's a visual image I didn't need."

He stared at the tips of his grass-stained sneakers. "I love it here."

"Me too." The ice jingled in the glass as she swirled the liquid. "Have you recovered from lunch?"

"Never." He rested his head against the back of the seat.

"It's good for you."

"So is pizza."

"Wrong."

Comfortable silence descended. In the past, this is when she unloaded and left. Just when he settled in, she got wanderlust.

As the days flipped by this time around, each one better than the one before, he waited for her to slam another door shut. He doubted he'd survive another round, but he couldn't hold back. He'd lose either way.

In his mind, they were together forever. When she accepted his invitation and walked into that bar, they'd made an unspoken deal. He didn't want anyone else. He was done with dating and looking. He didn't have to play the field.

He was forty. He'd seen a lot of life and knew the best parts led back to her. Whether she saw their life unfolding the same way was the question.

"Why do you do that?" she asked.

He opened his eyes and saw her staring at him. For a minute he thought he might have voiced his worries out loud. When she didn't yell or launch into a fight, he guessed it was something else.

"What?"

"Tense."

It sounded like she was throwing out words without context. "I'm not following this conversation."

"When we fall into these quiet times, and I come to sit with you, your shoulders tense. It's as if you're putting up a barrier against me."

Damn, she saw it. "Just your imagination."

Her face closed. "Don't do that."

He wasn't sure what to say or how to apologize for just sitting there. "Okay."

If the blow was coming, he wanted it to land and be done. Instead, she slipped her hand into his and leaned in as close as the big chairs would allow. "I'm not leaving."

This time his body jerked. "I . . ."

"That's it, right? You think I'm going to get bored and go. You are basing this time on what happened before, when we were kids."

"Not every time."

"We weren't mature. That was my point."

"It wouldn't be the first time you left."

Sadness dimmed her eyes. "Did I do this to you?"

He gave her fingers a gentle squeeze. "Let's let this go."

"I'm sorry."

The harsh whisper burned through him. "You didn't do anything wrong."

It took him years to come to that conclusion. For so many, he blamed her. She chased her dreams and forgot his. But then he watched other women in his life struggle as he failed to commit.

He developed dreams of his own. With that came an understanding that timing mattered. Not being ready was a real answer, not just a lame excuse to bolt.

"Paul, this is it." She lowered his head until he met her intense gaze head on. "Do you understand what I'm saying? I'm not looking for anything. I've found it."

"At Naked News."

She rolled her eyes. "With you."

"I never got that."

"What?"

He focused on the water as he spoke. "You were this beautiful, almost untouchable girl. You carried that into adulthood, becoming this smart and exhausting woman who zings from topic to topic and never rests."

"Guilty."

He turned back to her and asked the one question he wasn't sure he wanted her to answer. "Why me?"

"What?"

"I was a kid without a family, an adult without direction."

"Oh, Paul." She lifted there joint hands and brushed a kiss over his knuckles. "You found your way."

"You could have had anyone."

"It's always been you."

His insides caught fire when she talked like that. "I love you."

"And I love you."

But those feelings were there before. Unspoken, yes, but clear. He'd never doubted she loved him, and he knew he loved her. "Is it enough this time?"

"It's everything. There is no me without you."

The combination of her eyes and her death grip on his hand got through. She was willing him to get it. "You've found what you're looking for."

"With you. Here. Us."

The last of his fears slipped away. He leaned in close. "Let's go scare the dogs."

Christmas came fast that year. They'd been working and moving and making plans for the future. By the time everyone gathered at her parent's house, Jennifer was exhausted. She loved them but wanted them all out so she could snuggle with Paul.

The months leading up to the big day had been so perfect with Paul. They fed off each other's love, shared their dreams and nurtured their desires. Neither of them looked to a future without seeing the other.

They sat around the sunken living room with all the people who had come to mean so much to them both. They passed the wrapped packages to the right recipients. Everyone huddled and laughed. There was an over-abundance of coffee and sweet things that guaranteed to make them all hyper. It was a holiday after all.

Paul handed her a small box. "For you."

The noise in the room faded and all eyes grew huge. It was as if everyone held a collective breath once they saw the size of the package.

She didn't need to guess. She knew. She felt the unspoken question when she touched the box.

She tore into the paper and stared at the small velvet box. It was beautiful just like this. It didn't matter what was inside. It was all a symbol for something greater.

"Aren't you going to open it?" Paul joked.

She flipped the top open as her heartbeat thundered in her ears. If anyone was talking, she couldn't hear them. The moment narrowed to her and Paul and a pretty black box.

With a creak, the box revealed the perfect red ruby. Not a diamond. He wouldn't do that. He knew she wasn't a huge fan. No, this went deeper. It was one more example of how he understood her. All of her.

She stared up at him and knew. The ring was the question, so personal and private that he wouldn't say it in front of everyone.

She lifted it out of the box as everyone around them froze. When she slid it on, her gaze went to Paul's face. It was all written right there. His heart, his life, was in that ring. By wearing it, she was saying yes.

Without a word, she slipped into his arms and stayed there. The silent communication said everything. Or it did to them. When they turned to leave the room, her father spoke up.

"What does this mean?"

Paul never took his gaze from hers. "It means I love your daughter."

They left the family room with their hands linked. In silence, they walked along the train tracks that still ran behind her parents' home. They traveled this same path over the years. Like so many times before, they shuffled, enjoying the silence until one of them stepped in.

He stopped and faced her. "I love you."

Nothing felt better than hearing him say the words. "I know."

"The ring is a promise." He didn't get down on one knee. He spoke from the heart with a voice as clear as the wind.

She knew what he meant because she felt it, too. "It's forever."

"Forever." He kissed her then. Long and deep with a note that echoed the promise in their words. "I will do everything I can to make you happy. I will never hurt you or leave you. You're my everything."

She held his hands and repeated the words back to him. By the time they were done, she didn't need the big ceremony or official words.

In her mind, they were married. Bound together forever. She knew he felt the same way.

They were the only ones. Weeks after Christmas, notes congratulating them on the engagement started to arrive. With each envelope, Paul handed her the card and she hung it up. They never talked about a wedding, but everyone decided they were engaged.

Without an official announcement, she never thought this would be an issue. What was enough for them was a constant source of curiosity from their friends and family.

One day she and Paul sat with her two best friends, Andrea and Michelle, in the parlor of the new five-bedroom house she and Paul had bought in Toronto with an eye toward establishing roots. It was big and old and lovely. She adored every inch of the historical property.

As much as she loved the house and all that it stood for—stability and a future—the people around her meant so much more. Andrea and Michelle had stuck by her through everything, supported her and celebrated her joys. They were the friends every woman needed and deserved.

And it was clear they were on a mission today. They sat on either side of Paul. The poor guy didn't stand a chance.

The breakfast dishes clanked as Andrea passed a plate to Paul. "So, about the ring."

He frowned. "Don't you start."

Michelle patted Paul's arm. "You'll thank us for this one day."

Jennifer knew what he was thinking. He wanted decisions about where they went from here to remain private and couldn't understand why all of these people cared so much. He was a guy, but really, she agreed. She didn't need a rush to the altar. Being engaged suited her.

Andrea and Michelle apparently disagreed.

"Do you have it?" Andrea asked as she held her hand out across the table in Michelle's general direction.

Michelle dragged out a calendar from her bag and set it on the edge of the table. "Here you go."

Studying the pages, Andrea glanced around the table. "What are you two doing on September ninth?"

Jennifer looked at Paul and saw his eyes sparkle. He wasn't angry. He'd long ago learned that Andrea was a whirlwind and Michelle was the perfect sidekick, and he took it in stride.

"Getting married?" Jennifer suggested.

"Right." Andrea inked a big circle around the ninth day of month nine. "It's a date."

Michelle smiled. "Now we can eat."

Thirty

Love is only the beginning.

—Grandma Gladys, The Duchess

IT WAS THE WEEK BEFORE THEIR WEDDING, AND PAUL hadn't suffered one second of jitters. His only regret was that it had taken so long to get here.

He used the time while Jennifer shopped for dresses and a host of other activities he didn't care about at all to get everything in order. She could handle the details. He was counting down the days to the honeymoon.

And getting his life in order. That took more time than he expected.

Leaving his job was the toughest part. Not that he was so attached to it. But living in Toronto and sticking close to Jennifer instead of heading out for six months a year meant finding a nine-to-five job. Suits and ties. Rules and bosses who screamed for no reason.

He hated all of it. It caused his mind to shut down. He felt it but couldn't stop it.

To escape, he fell into his photography with even more excitement. Even now he shuffled the photos he'd taken last week. Private ones. Jennifer in the bedroom. Nothing tacky. This was pure art. They unwrapped her soul through her eyes and her body.

For the first time, she let go of everything and stopped posing as she'd been taught at Naked News. This wasn't about getting the perfect shot. He wanted the right one. The one that uncovered a piece of her.

He'd succeeded. These were real and genuine. They captured the sweet, sexy, complicated woman she was.

She came up behind him and slid her arms around his waist. "What are you doing?"

"Running away from home until the caterer stops calling."

"Well, you're going to have to take me with you because if I hear about one more floral arrangement—" She stopped, her hand going to the stack of black and white photos he hadn't checked out yet. "These are of me."

"Funny thing, but the lady next door refuses to strip and let me photograph her."

"That's not what I mean." She pivoted around him and paged through the papers as if in a trance.

The reaction scared the hell out of him. He'd poured every emotion and bit of energy into this work. If she shot it down, she'd slam him at a fundamental level.

"I know they're not professional quality—"

She turned to him with tears in her eyes and a photo clenched to her chest. "It's not that."

"Jennifer."

"Don't you see?"

"If you hate them I can get rid of them." It would kill him, but he'd do it to spare her any distress.

"Don't you dare." She yelled the warning.

Now she had him all turned around. He didn't understand what was setting off this reaction or what the reaction even meant. "I don't—"

"You see it all." She stared at the photo that had been trapped against her sweater. "You captured Jennifer and Victoria. Both at the same time."

The hot ball of tension in his gut fizzled out. "They're both in you."

"But I can see them." She pointed to the photo. "It's as if you dragged both aspects out of me and placed them on the page with a gentle hand."

"I didn't do anything."

She treated him to a watery smile. "You see me. All of me."

"Of course."

"No, don't act like that's usual. It's rare. Most people don't see it."

He caressed her jaw. "The one thing I am is an expert on you."

She pressed a soft kiss on his mouth. "Can I have this?"

"I can do a better copy."

"No, this one."

"Sure."

She walked out of the room but stopped in the doorway to face him. "Paul?"

"Yeah, babe?"

"I'm so happy I'm marrying you."

Epilogue

A YEAR LATER JENNIFER LOOKED OUT THE WINDOW over the kitchen sink of the main house. Her husband walked up the ladder at the side of Cabin Five. When he got to the top rung, he stripped off his shirt.

She loved this part. Seeing him outside, his mind focused on the job . . . and his tanned chest gleaming in the sunshine. After leaving his job to move in with her and get married, he took a new job. A desk job. He'd been miserable trapped inside—until that day they went to the cottage at Lake Orr for a getaway and saw the sale sign. A seventy-acre park, the Green Acres RV Park. Derelict cabins and grounds that needed work.

The job suited him. Suited both of them. The reality of getting older made her look outside Naked News for future answers. She still worked there and loved every minute, but her focus had shifted.

They signed the paperwork, and she shipped Paul and the dogs up there to get working right after they got back home. She'd stayed behind to sell their house in Toronto. The relocation went smoothly.

Running the park was a different story.

Now their evenings were spent making plans to update the park and add new cabins. Paul had to fix the ones they had first, which meant long hours of tough work. And there was always something new to fix.

She watched the sun set his skin aglow. He thrived in this environment. He'd come alive as the responsibility piled on top of him.

Between the PR work and managing this place, she was exhausted, but it was a good type of exhaustion. The type that came from a hard day of work and a hot night of passion.

With the phone quiet and her computer work caught up, she decided to take a nap. She never indulged, but having her head hit the pillow sounded so good.

She had just drifted off to sleep when she felt Paul's hand on her shoulder. She rolled over thinking he wanted to take advantage of the bed. "Hi there." "Do you know the nonemergency number for the police?" She did a straight-up jackknife. "What?"

"I've got it under control. Just need the number."

She debated an interrogation until he gave her the details, but then she saw his face. Determined and calm. A deep inhale slowed her rampaging heartbeat. "You can handle it."

He smiled. "Of course." Her trust in him never wavered. "It's on the speed dial."

Patting her bottom, he headed for the door. "Go back to sleep." Easy for him to say. She fell back against the mattress. Her mind spun with the theories about what was happening out there. He either found something or saw something.

She stared at the ceiling. She trusted him but that didn't mean she was the type of person who could lounge around after hearing that news. She slid her legs over the side of the bed. She'd just put her shoes on when his head popped up in the doorway.

His chuckle filled the room. "I'm amazed it took you that long to get up and come snooping."

"I totally trust you."

"I know." He reached his hand out. "Come on. We'll handle it together."

"Together." She slid her fingers through his, sealing the connection. "I like that."

"And I like you. A lot." He squeezed her hand. But it was that roguish grin of his that got her every time and could still make her skin tingle like it did when they were kids making out in the backseat of a car.

The feeling lingered as they put out the latest little fire at their Green Acres RV park. *Their* RV park. And *their* waterfront cottage, which they had dubbed "Kingfisher." Arm-in-arm they surveyed it together. Jennifer pulled a stray weed from the well-tended lawn as they rounded the pristine charmer that Paul had so beautifully renovated. Inside and out. A lot like the magic his steadfast love had worked on her.

"M'lady? Your chariot awaits." With a flourish he swept an arm towards their pontoon, tethered to the wharf he had recently rebuilt with good, sturdy wood. The new wood was pretty and still yellow, yet to show signs of storms weathered on the sandy shores of Lake Orr.

The water glistened. So beautiful and peaceful, their own private oasis—all the more appreciated after the storms they had managed to weather together. As Paul untied the rope with his strong, capable hands, then gave a healthy shove to set them afloat, Jennifer surveyed the bounty before her. An embarrassment of riches, The Duchess would say.

The Duchess was right.

Submit Your Own True Romance Story

"The marriage of real-life stories with classic, fictional romance—an amazing concept."

—**Peggy Webb**, award-winning author of sixty romance novels

Do you have the greatest love story never told? A sexy, steamy, bigger-than-life or just plain worthwhile love story to tell?

If so, then here's your chance to share it with us. Your true romance may possibly be selected as the basis for the next book in the TRUE VOWS series, the first-ever Reality-Based Romance™ series.

- Did you meet the love of your life under unusual circumstances that defy the laws of nature and/or have a relationship that flourished against all odds of making it to the altar?
- Did your parents tell you a story so remarkable about themselves that it makes you feel lucky to have ever been born?
- Are you a military wife who stood by her man while he was oceans away, held down the fort at home, then had to rediscover each other upon his return?
- Did you lose a great love and think you would never survive, only for fate to deliver an embarrassment of riches a second or even third time around?

Story submissions are reviewed by TRUE VOWS editors, who are always on the lookout for the next TRUE VOWS Romance.

Visit www.truevowsbooks.com to tell us your true romance.

True Vows. It's Life . . . Romanticized

Sexy, Entertaining, Inspiring, and Based on True Romances

Code 5682 • Paperback • $13.95

Bestselling romance author Tara Taylor Quinn dares to novelize her own true love story filled with heartbreaking truths. This groundbreaking novel offers a soaring message of hope that the redeeming power of love can truly conquer all.

www.truevowsbooks.com

More from *True Vows*™
Reality-Based Romances

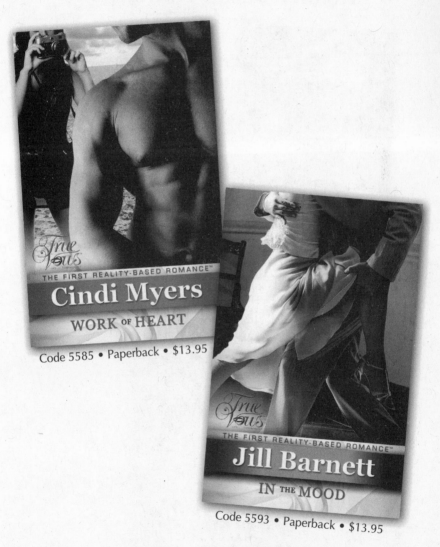

Code 5585 • Paperback • $13.95

Code 5593 • Paperback • $13.95

www.truevowsbooks.com

Get Ready to Be Swept Away...
By More *True Vows*™
Reality-based Romances